PRIDE
OF THE
PEACOCK

THE
PITTSBURGH
PEACE
INSTITUTE

PRIDE
OF THE
PEACOCK

Stephanie S. Tolan

CHARLES SCRIBNER'S SONS

NEW YORK

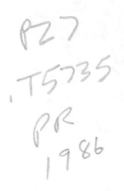
Words from "Bridge Over Troubled Water"
on page 175 copyright © 1969 Paul Simon.
Used by permission.

Copyright © 1986 Stephanie S. Tolan

Library of Congress Cataloging-in-Publication Data
Tolan, Stephanie S.   Pride of the peacock.
Summary: After reading a book describing the
aftermath of a nuclear war, fourteen-year-old
Whitney becomes obsessed with the inevitability
of the earth's destruction and finds herself more
and more paralyzed by fear and depression.
[1. Nuclear warfare—Fiction.   2. Fear—Fiction.
3. Friendship—Fiction]   I. Title.
PZ7.T5735Pr   1985   [Fic]   85-40290
ISBN 0-684-18489-3

1 3 5 7 9 11 13 15 17 19   FG/C   20 18 16 14 12 10 8 6 4 2

Printed in the United States of America

For Katherine Paterson,
story-teller
lighter of candles
bridge over troubled water

❦ 1 ❦

Whitney put the book carefully on top of the pile of school-books on her desk. She handled it as if it were a ticking time bomb, as if it would explode if she jolted it. The blue-green cover with its white letters looked innocent enough. *The Fate of the Earth*, the letters said. Then two heavy white lines, then the author's name: Jonathan Schell. Just an ordinary paperback book. Its spine and front cover were creased from handling, and along the creases the shiny color had cracked, so that there were thin white lines across the white letters. It looked a little as if someone had drawn lines through the title and the author's name, trying to cross them out. Whitney wished someone had. She wished someone had crossed out the whole book, even the idea of the book as it had begun in the author's mind. But it wouldn't really make any difference. It wasn't the book's fault. It wasn't the author's fault. If only she, Whitney Whitehurst, hadn't read it. She wasn't ready for it. The trouble was, she had read it, and nothing would ever be the same again.

She sat on her bed and leaned back into the pillows she had propped against the headboard while she read. Then she pulled her knees up under her chin and wrapped her arms around them. She was shivering. The light from her

1

reading lamp fell across her striped comforter, and suddenly everything seemed too bright, the primary colors of the stripes too cheerful. Whitney turned off the lamp. Darkness swallowed her room. The yellow slatted blinds over her windows were closed and so was her door. She held her hand in front of her face and couldn't see it. Good. She didn't want to see anything—especially not that book.

She tried to concentrate on the sounds in the house around her, normal sounds of normal life. She could hear a faint clattering from the kitchen that meant Kate was finally doing the dishes. Kate always left them as long as she dared when it was her turn, probably hoping that someone else would give in and do them if she waited long enough. Nobody ever did. The television was on in the living room, which meant that their mother was watching a movie. Marianne Whitehurst was a prime-time television addict. Their father, a professor of biology at Martinsville State, would be in his study working on the textbook he was writing. And Whitney's four-year-old brother, Jeremy, would be asleep in the room next to her own. In Jeremy's room it wouldn't be dark, because Jeremy was terrified of the dark. His room, its floor strewn with blocks and Legos and Fisher-Price toys, would be glowing a soft blue from the man-in-the-moon lamp on his dresser. Whitney knew exactly how her brother looked at this moment. His hair would be damp around his face because for some reason he always perspired when he slept. And one arm would be tightly wrapped around his potbellied bear.

It was intolerable that Jeremy should live in the dangerous, horrible world Jonathan Schell had written about. It was intolerable that the fate of the earth would also be the fate of Jeremy Whitehurst.

Whitney wished she had a dog. Right this minute it would be good to have a dog. He would be a big, shaggy, bumbling idiot of a dog whose name would be Fred, and he would sleep on her bed with her. Right now he could be stretched out next to her, his warm body against hers, his breath going in and out noisily as he slept. Having a warm body against her, hearing something breathing, might help her stop shivering. It might help her believe that life would go on and on, eons and eons of it. But there was no Whitehurst dog. There was only an aquarium full of guppies downstairs on the dining room buffet. Somehow, she was sure, even if they were right there in her room, guppies wouldn't make her feel any better.

It didn't seem really dark anymore, now that her eyes had adjusted. There was light coming in around the edges of her door, and the numbers on her alarm clock were glowing an insistent green, telling her that it was ten thirty-seven. Bedtime. She couldn't imagine being able to sleep. All her muscles seemed to have tensed up. Her mother complained about stress and tension all the time. This must be what it felt like. It was the way a rubber band got when you twisted it 'round and 'round and 'round until it coiled back on itself and got shorter and shorter. Whitney thought she was probably three inches shorter right now, just from all that tension. She might snap any minute.

Footsteps went past her door. Kate must have finished the dishes. She'd be going to her room to finish her home-

3

work and set her hair and put cream on her face and then, last of all, write in her diary. As far as Whitney knew, Kate had never failed to finish her homework and in four years had never missed writing in her diary. Four fat volumes, each a different color, each firmly locked, sat on the top shelf of Kate's bookcase. That wasn't the only thing Kate wrote—she wrote poetry, too. And played the flute. Slim and ethereal-looking, she was exactly the opposite of chunky, freckled Whitney. A lot of good it was to be slim and ethereal, Whitney thought, or to record what happened every day. Kate had explained once that she wrote in her diary so that when she grew up she could look back and remember what her life had been like. What was the point, then, if the world was going to blow up? Kate would never be grown-up and would never be able to read those fat diaries. What was the point of anything? Of poetry or playing the flute or putting on face cream? What was the point of homework if nobody was going to grow up to use an education?

Whitney hadn't done any of her own homework tonight. Her math book lay untouched in the pile underneath *The Fate of the Earth* along with the science lab report she was supposed to have copied over. She'd done nothing but read since she got home from school. Had she even gone downstairs for supper? She couldn't remember what they'd had or whether she'd eaten. What was wrong with her brain? She had to have eaten or everybody would have yelled, and there hadn't been any yelling.

Dinner. She remembered now that she'd put down the book when her father had pounded on her door, and she'd gone downstairs like a zombie. There'd been the usual talk around the table, something about Kate's boyfriend, Gordon, something about the finger painting Jeremy had brought home from the day-care center. But Whitney hadn't really been there. She'd been thinking about thousands and millions and zillions of human beings that would never get a chance to live at all when the human race became extinct. She'd imagined them like wispy ghost babies stretched in a long line going into the sky, waiting to be born. But they never would be—there would be no more babies, ever. And while everybody else in the Whitehurst family had chatted and eaten whatever it was they were eating, she'd spooned food mechanically into her mouth until her plate was empty and she could get back to her room to go on reading.

She knew she didn't understand everything in the book, but she understood enough. Russia and the United States were planning for a nuclear war, getting closer and closer to it every single day, making more and more nuclear weapons. Every day the chance for war got greater and the time for stopping it got shorter. She'd kept on reading, because she was sure at the end of the book there would be an answer, the thing that would save her and everybody else and the earth. But the author didn't have the answer. He didn't even say for sure there was one.

Whitney shivered again. Without taking off her jeans or her blouse or even her loafers, she pulled her comforter up and over her. She curled herself into a tight ball and buried her face in her pillow, but she couldn't stop shivering.

The alarm was making its horrible buzzing sound. Whitney opened her eyes and closed them again. She'd been in the middle of a wonderful dream, though she couldn't remember now what it had been about. If she could only get back to sleep, it would be there again. But the buzzing went through her head like a drill. She batted at the top of the clock until she hit the button that would stop the noise and sighed. Why did she have to be in the middle of a dream every time that thing went off? She pulled her comforter up under her chin and tried to snuggle back into her pillow. The taste of that dream in her mind was like the aftertaste of fudge on her tongue, sweet and demanding.

After a minute, she opened her eyes again. Daylight poured in around the blinds. It was no use. The dream was gone forever. Whitney sat up, threw off her comforter, and stared down at herself in amazement. She was fully dressed. She even had on her shoes. Her mind stumbled around the edges of being awake, and then, as if a spinning coin had fallen over and stopped, she remembered. That book. She'd finished it and nearly scared herself to death. *The Fate of the Earth*. Destruction. Nuclear holocaust. Whitney shivered again, remembering. Even more than before, she wished she could go back to sleep and take refuge in a good dream.

She swung her legs over the edge of the bed. The light forcing its way in stripes through the blinds was as yellow as the blinds. It would be a beautiful, sunny spring day. Whitney stretched, yawned, and stood up. She wished it were raining and miserable out. She wished it were February. It wouldn't be so awful to think about the end of the world in February. She went to a window and lifted one slat of the blind. Sunlight poured in and she blinked. Outside, the grass was getting tall. The new, small leaves on the trees were that fresh, yellowy green that meant rebirth, growing—billions of tiny chlorophyll factories beginning to manufacture food from the energy of the sun. The sun—God's thermonuclear device. One of them, she corrected herself. The stars were all continuous nuclear explosions. She let the slat fall back into place. The gloom of her room was more comfortable than the brightness outside.

"Whitney, did you borrow my pink cardigan again?" Kate knocked on Whitney's door and then stuck her head into the room. "I wish you'd ask before you borrow my things."

Whitney shook her head. "I didn't borrow it."

Kate squinted at her and then flipped on the overhead light. "For heaven's sake, Whit, you look like you slept in that blouse! You aren't going to school like that, I hope. If you'd turn on a light so you could see what you were putting on, you wouldn't end up looking like some rag-picker's kid or something. And couldn't you wear a skirt for a change? Half the world probably thinks I have two brothers. Are you absolutely sure you don't have my pink cardigan?" Whitney shook her head. "Well, where is it then?" Kate asked no one in particular, and slammed the door.

Whitney could hear the steady whine of her father's shaver coming from the master bathroom. Next door, Jeremy had launched into his favorite song. "Do your ears hang low, do they wobble to and fro?" he sang. For some reason, he thought these were the funniest words he'd ever heard. "Can you tie them in a knot, can you tie them in a bow?" Giggles were creeping in, but he managed to go on. "Can you throw them o'er your shoulder like a Continental soldier? Do your ears hang low?" His voice dissolved into helpless laughter. It didn't matter how often he sang it, the song always cracked him up. Whitney grinned. It was almost impossible not to laugh when Jeremy did. Marianne Whitehurst said that if they could figure out how to bottle that laugh, they'd all be rich. Down the hall, Kate was loudly opening and closing drawers and cursing. She wasn't sounding very poetic this morning, Whitney thought.

The smell of coffee drifted up from the kitchen. The coffee maker had a timer, so it started all by itself. In a way, it was the first member of the Whitehurst household to get up every morning. Marianne, who worked at a bank, always got up at the last minute, then rushed around trying to get her makeup on and her hair done while being sure everyone else left the house on time as well. Mornings were not Marianne Whitehurst's favorite time.

It was, Whitney thought, a completely typical morning. The thought was not comforting. It brought back the memory of the books she had read in the fall about Great American Disasters. Every single book in the series had begun on a typical morning. The author would describe some typical family beginning some typical day, shaving, singing songs, making coffee, worrying about things like pink cardigans. Only the author and the reader, knowing what was to come, understood the irony of it all. Only the author and the reader knew that by two o'clock that very afternoon the adorable four-year-old who at seven-fifteen had laughed about someone's ears hanging low would have been blown away by a tornado or buried under a mud slide or burned to a cinder in a fire that engulfed the whole town. Only the author and the reader knew that wherever the pink cardigan might be, the poetry-writing flute player would never need it again.

Those books had been like salted peanuts. Whitney had gone through one right after another until she'd finished the whole series. All the major disasters had been done, it seemed —fires and tornados and hurricanes, volcanos and mud slides, floods and ship sinkings, earthquakes and blizzards and epidemics. She wasn't sure what it was she liked about them so much. But there was something fascinating about knowing, as she hopped with the author from household to household in the opening pages, getting to know all those unsuspecting people, that their lives were about to be snuffed out or changed forever by something they couldn't do anything about. Of course, *some* of them would be spared, when the mud slide hit a huge rock and went miraculously around them or when the tornado skipped up and over the spot where they were standing or when a heroic fireman dragged them out of a building mere seconds before it exploded. It was fun to try to figure out, at the beginning, who would be the ones to survive. She could usually tell by the way the author described the person. The cuter or funnier or nicer the person, the less likely he'd be to survive. Jeremy, for instance, would never make it.

Her friend Allie said it was grotesque and unnatural to like reading about catastrophes. Whitney paid very little attention because Allie was forever reading romance novels and had no room to criticize anybody. Sometimes she told Allie that it was educationally sound and good for her character to read those books, because she always tried to figure out what she would do in one of those situations. Would she be one of the heroic ones or one of the cowards? Would she be clever enough to see the disaster coming and get ready? Would she be crafty or strong or brave enough to survive? Usually she cried when characters in the book were killed, or even when they were spared and reunited with worried relatives and friends. The tears were part of it, though, and she had read on, keeping a box of Kleenex handy, until she'd finally finished every book in the series. Then she'd read two of the more exciting ones again.

Maybe, Whitney thought now, she liked those books so well because no matter how dreadful the disaster was, the reader was always perfectly safe. While those actual people (the books were all nonfiction, of course) were being destroyed in front of her eyes, she was warm and comfortable in the reclining chair in her father's study with a cup of cocoa on the table next to her and maybe a plate of cookies or a pair of Twinkies to eat. As a character dug through rubble, hoping to salvage a crust of bread to save him from starvation, she would be licking the cream center off her fingers in preparation for turning the page.

Now those books came back to haunt her. She had the uncomfortable sense that somewhere a reader was licking her fingers and turning pages in the story of Whitney White-hurst—in the story of the end of the planet earth and all the life that inhabited it. Whitney was no more than one of those unsuspecting characters about to be wiped out. Somewhere someone was reading about her standing in her bedroom in yesterday's clothes. Someone was reading about Allie Hamilton, eating her breakfast and getting ready to come pick Whitney up, and about Paul Forest, probably sitting on his rumpled bed amidst a pile of dirty clothes trying to decide which sweat shirt to wear to school. Somewhere someone was smiling at the effort her father had put into working on his textbook last night, knowing that it would never get published. This time it didn't matter whether the characters were cute or funny or nice, because this time nobody was going to be spared. There weren't going to be any survivors.

Whitney kicked off her loafers and went back to bed. The blue-green book seemed to be grinning at her from her desk. She glared at it. Maybe she could change everything if she refused to let this be a typical day. She'd revolt. And that reader (she imagined her to be a girl like herself, though in some weird science-fictiony room in another universe) would be robbed of the thrilling irony. Whitney Whitehurst wouldn't be innocent and unsuspecting. She would refuse to be a victim, or let the earth be a victim either, for that matter. Right now there were satellites, circling the earth with their electronic systems watching for the telltale signs of missiles being launched. Well, let them circle. Today wouldn't be the day. Whitney Whitehurst wouldn't let it be.

"Whitney, honey," her mother's voice called from down the hall, "are you dressed? Would you get Jeremy's cereal ready for him? I'm running late."

"Can't, Mom," Whitney yelled back. "I'm sick. I'm staying in bed today."

Moments later, her mother appeared in the doorway of

11

her room, a hairbrush in one hand, her reddish-brown hair only half pinned into the businesslike twist she was wearing these days. "What's the matter, Whit? Do you have a fever?"

Whitney tried looking pale. "I don't think so. Maybe it's stomach flu. I feel rotten in my middle."

"I knew something was wrong last night when you didn't ask for seconds of taco pie. And you didn't even have sour cream on it."

"There was sour cream? When did you start buying sour cream again?"

"Oh, I didn't really start buying it again. I just saw it at the store and thought it might be nice to have it, this once. I'd have let you have some, if you'd asked, but you never asked. I just knew something was the matter."

Whitney frowned. If she'd had to be so out of it that she didn't even know what she was eating, why did it have to be taco pie? With sour cream? "I guess I must have been getting sick last night. Is it okay if I stay home today?"

"I guess so. I hate to leave you when you're sick. Will you be all right? You want me to come home on my lunch hour?"

"No thanks. I think I'll just sleep."

Whitney couldn't help noticing that her mother looked relieved as she left. There was nothing she hated worse than having to come home in the middle of the day. Even for Jeremy.

Staying in bed wouldn't really change anything, Whitney thought with a sigh. If the missiles were going to fly today, they'd fly anyway. Probably they wouldn't, of course. Not yet. Soon, but not yet. At least, if she stayed in bed, she wouldn't have to look at the spring world beginning again and wonder if it was worth it. At least she wouldn't be in school, where everything they learned was supposed to do them some good in the future, wondering how much future was left. Bed was as good a hiding place as any. She pulled her comforter up around her shoulders and beat her pillow into a ball. Then she snuggled down and closed her eyes. She would not think about the fate of anything anymore. And maybe she'd have another good dream.

❦ 2 ❦

"Hey in there, WhitWurst! What's the matter?"

"Allie? What're you doing up here?"

"I've come to sit by your sickbed. For exactly six minutes, and then I have to go or I'll miss the bus. Is it really stomach flu? Because if it is, I'm going to stay out here with the door between us."

"Some friend."

"There's a limit to friendship, Whit. I loathe vomiting."

"Who doesn't? Is Mom still home? Or Dad?"

"Your mom and Jeremy were leaving just as I got here. She barely stopped long enough to tell me about your stomach flu. I don't know about the Professor. I didn't see him."

"Come in."

"What about the flu?"

"I said, come in, Allie. You will not catch stomach flu from me. I promise."

Allie Hamilton opened the door cautiously and looked in. "How can you promise? That stuff spreads like . . ."

"Because I don't have stomach flu. Now get in here and close the door. My dad may be out there somewhere."

Allie came in, closed the door, and set her backpack on the

floor. She stayed where she was, leaning against the wall. "Then what do you have? Is it catching?"

Whitney frowned. "Not the way you mean. I'm not sick. Repeat, not sick. At least not physically. You don't have to stay clear over there."

"So what are you doing, just skipping school?"

Whitney shrugged. "I guess so. You could put it that way."

"Mr. Jackson'll have a kitten if you don't turn in your lab report. It'll be the third time you've been late this nine weeks."

"It doesn't matter."

"Yeah? Tell him that."

"Listen, Allie, I mean it. It doesn't matter. *Nothing* matters. Not science, not math, not language arts or social studies or even whether anyone asks you to the spring ball."

The braces glinted in Allie's open mouth. "What are you talking about? Are you having another one of your catastrophe obsessions? What is it this time—toxic wastes? Arsenic in the well water?" She came across to the edge of the bed, moving in that loose-jointed way she'd had since her arms and legs had grown so suddenly. She sat down on the corner of the bed, her long, thin legs stretched out across Whitney's yellow rug. For the third day in a row she was wearing a skirt. Junior high was rotting Allie's brain, Whitney thought. If it went on like this, they'd have nothing in common at all. Their friendship would be a thing of the past. As if that mattered. Everything was going to be a thing of the past.

"Well?" Allie glanced at her watch. "I don't have long. Are you going to tell me or not?"

"This is different. Really it is."

15

Allie sighed and pushed a stray lock of blond hair behind her ear. "It's always different. Every single thing you've gotten hooked on this whole year has been 'different.' Even your parents' getting a divorce, which I could point out, is anything but different. And which, I could also point out, wasn't happening in the first place."

"Those things were all little compared to this."

"*Now* you say that. You didn't think that divorce business was so little at the time. You wanted to take Jeremy and run away. If I remember correctly, you spent your entire savings on bus tickets."

Whitney sat up. "Well, it would have been a great plan if they *had* been planning a divorce. They'd have had to get together to find us. You said yourself it was a good idea."

"Yeah, well, you were very persuasive. Anyway, they weren't even thinking about a divorce."

"So they said. I still think they'd been considering it—in the back of their minds."

"So what's up now? And why are you in bed with your clothes on? Isn't that the blouse you wore yesterday?"

"Yes. Never mind about that. This is really serious. There's nothing in the world as serious as this—not PCBs or arsenic in the water, not acid rain, not toxic wastes, and certainly not divorce. I've just finished reading *The Fate of the Earth.*"

"That book you're doing for your nonfiction book report?"

"Yes! It's about nuclear war."

"I thought it was another one of those ecology things."

"No. Now listen carefully, Allie. The human race is going to be extinct!"

"Everybody knows that, Whitney. If they push the button

16

nobody'll be left except some Indian tribes in South America or Australia or something."

"Extinct, Allie! Like the dinosaurs. And dodo birds. *All gone.* There aren't going to be any Indians or any Australians or anybody else. We're all going to die out. And with us will go all the birds and probably all the mammals and just about everything else except maybe some bugs and some creatures that live way at the bottom of the oceans."

Allie looked at her watch again and unfolded herself until she stood looking down on Whitney. "I have to get going. No one's home to take me to school if I miss the bus. What're you planning to do? Stay in bed until Russia launches its missiles?"

"I don't know what I'm going to do."

"Well, do you want me to tell anybody at school anything? Are you sticking with the stomach flu story?"

"Never mind." How was she going to get anyone to listen to her if Allie wouldn't? Nobody would care. Nobody wanted to look past today. But it was so frustrating! Like yelling at someone that a tree was falling and having the person just stand there. Whitney sighed. What difference did it make, anyway? You could jump out of the way of a falling tree, but you couldn't very well jump off the earth and go somewhere else till the danger was over. "I wish you'd just read the book, at least, so you'd see what I mean."

Allie went over to Whitney's dresser and bent to find a clear space on the mirror to check her hair. "I wish you wouldn't cover your mirror with all these postcards and junk. I'd at least like to be able to see my whole face at once."

"Allie!"

17

"I don't *want* to read the book, Whitney. I don't want to read about mushroom clouds and fallout and people being vaporized. I have enough to worry about with my braces being too tight and my body being too tall and skinny and not having breasts. If we're all going to go bang, at least I want one heavy date before it happens. I just don't think it's going to happen before the spring ball, you know?"

Whitney flopped down again and pulled her comforter completely over her head. "You're going to miss the bus," she said from under it.

"What?"

"*You're going to miss the bus!*"

"Right. You'll get over this, Whit. You just can't go around worrying about the end of the world. Life's too . . ." Allie giggled. "I was just going to say 'Life's too short.' Not exactly what you want to hear, huh? I'll come over after school. Maybe you'll be feeling better by then."

Whitney didn't move until she'd heard the door close, and then she merely uncovered her face so she could breathe. She wished she could make Allie understand. It wasn't a joking matter. Even if there wasn't anything either of them could do to stop what was happening in the world, she wished that at least she had someone to talk to about it, someone who wouldn't make fun of the fear.

Of course she'd been scared before. Sometimes she had the feeling that nobody in the world was as cowardly as she was. There was always something. But she wasn't imagining the things she was scared of. They were real. Toxic waste dumps really did kill—people were dying of cancer and all sorts of other diseases because poisons were leaking out of old metal

18

containers. And there really were PCBs in rivers and in fish that people caught and ate. And gasoline really was leaking into people's drinking water. And just last month she'd read that the greenhouse effect was real, and not just some scientist's crazy prediction. The climate of the earth really was changing, and that could interfere with crops, and lots more people would starve even than the ones who were starving now. Her Encyclopedia Brown weird facts book said that already four people starved to death somewhere in the world in the time it took to read twenty-five words. It would get worse. Was she crazy because she remembered stuff like that and worried about it, or were the other people in the world crazy for ignoring it?

This terror wiped out all the others, of course. When nuclear war put an end to people and civilization, it would automatically end all the other problems. The whole planet would be a toxic waste dump.

This fear was the worst she'd ever felt. It was even worse than the time she'd thought she had leukemia. That time she'd been sure she was dying. She'd expected to have to have chemotherapy and lose her hair, and then, maybe after a short time when people thought she was in remission, suddenly it would get bad again and she'd die. The symptoms of leukemia were absolutely there. She'd noticed them the very day after a TV special on leukemia. When they were running laps during gym class, she'd gotten tired much faster than any of the other kids, and she'd had to stop before anyone else did. Fatigue and weakness were definite symptoms.

That time had really been the worst before this. She'd thought a lot about how sad it was that she'd never live

19

beyond childhood, how sad that her own brother probably wouldn't even remember her when he grew up. She'd even written out a will so everyone would know what to do with her things.

One night she'd sat and looked in the mirror for about half an hour, wondering what her face would look like when she died and if her eyes would get that glazed, empty look her guinea pig's eyes had had when she'd found it dead in the bottom of its cage that time. She'd wondered what her skull looked like. It was hard to believe that under her round, freckled face and red hair there was just an ordinary skull that probably looked just like any other skull in the world. Like the skull that held pencils on her father's desk. When she'd thought of that, she'd looked in the mirror and decided she could detect the bony outlines under her skin. That night she'd covered almost all of her mirror with postcards and stickers. She hadn't wanted to look at herself ever again. She'd kept thinking about dying, even after her mother told her that it wasn't leukemia that kept her from running as far as the other kids, it was all the ice cream and Twinkies. The idea of dying was still with her a lot.

But thinking about extinction was worse. That will she'd made, for instance. There wasn't any point in wills anymore. There wouldn't be anyone left to leave anything to. There wouldn't be any cemeteries either. No stones with names and dates and no one to read the names and dates or leave flowers or remember. Whitney thought of all the times she'd heard somebody on television talking about a person who'd died. They said things like "He'll always live in our memories." Or "Her life will go on because her work goes on." Or "He died for the cause of freedom." How could people deal with death when there'd be no one to remember, no work that could go on, no causes, no people who would live afterward? It wouldn't be individual death anymore, while the human race went on—it would be total death.

Mrs. Fanzio had told them in language arts about how important it was to see whether a writer outlasted his time. Like Shakespeare. You knew Shakespeare was a great writer because four hundred years after he'd written his plays, people still performed them, still liked them. If there was a writer somewhere writing a play this very moment, Whitney thought, no one would ever know if he was great, because there wouldn't be anyone around in four hundred years to read his plays. No one to act in them. No one to see them acted. No theaters. So what did being a great writer mean, anyway? In a whole universe without life, being a writer, being anything, couldn't count once people were gone.

Paul was taking Latin. Paul loved Latin. He said it was neat to learn a dead language, knowing that no one was alive who had ever heard it spoken by regular people. Next, he wanted to take Ancient Greek. Paul was the smartest person Whitney knew—maybe even a genius. But what good did it do to be a genius who knew a dead language? Pretty soon all languages would be dead, and all geniuses with them. And there wouldn't be anyone even to wonder about them. There'd be no anthropologists or archaeologists to care about trying to figure out things like when human beings started walking on two legs, or when their brains developed. There'd be no one in the universe who'd even remember that human beings had existed. All those years of civilization gone without even

21

anyone to be sorry. All that history just wiped out. Poof. Not only would there be nothing more left of people than there was of dinosaurs, but there wouldn't even be any intelligent life to find fossils and wonder. Nothing but a bare, dead, poisoned planet whirling around in the darkness and loneliness of space.

Whitney wasn't just shivering anymore. She was crying.

❦ 3 ❦

It had not been a good morning. Whitney hadn't been tired enough to sleep, and lying in bed, even with the quilt over her head, didn't keep her from thinking. By nine-thirty, she'd had to get up and get dressed. Then she'd gone down to the kitchen for breakfast. While she was fixing herself a batch of French toast and eating, she was able to keep her mind off bombs. But even she couldn't eat all morning. Next, she'd tried watching game shows. Seeing all those people get so excited about winning a car or a trip to the Bahamas just made her feel worse. "Enjoy it while you can," she told them. "At least you may never have to pay the taxes." Soap operas weren't any better. Questions like whose baby was whose or who was getting a divorce, or even who'd killed whose lover in a moment of insanity seemed suddenly too trivial to bother about. After that, she tried watching "Sesame Street," which only reminded her that the little kids learning to count wouldn't have time to grow up. Then she had a vision of Big Bird's yellow feathers on fire, and she turned off the set.

She tried the transcendental meditation techniques Kate had taught her, sitting cross-legged on the living room floor with her eyes closed, chanting "Ooohm" over and over. Kate had said that the chanting would keep thoughts from forming in her mind and would let everything go blank. Well, it kept word thoughts from forming pretty well, but didn't do a thing about pictures. Mushroom clouds came right through.

Sitting on the back porch was no better. She watched the chickadees and sparrows for a while and then got to feeling sorry for them. It wasn't their fault people had made missiles, but they'd be destroyed anyway. She went back into the house and did all the breakfast dishes. Then she washed the top of the stove and cleaned all the counters and emptied the crumbs out of the toaster. And finally, it was time for lunch. .

Leftover taco pie with plenty of sour cream kept her mind focused on eating. It was a good thing, she decided, that her mother didn't like to come home during the day. It would be hard to explain how, in the throes of stomach flu, she'd been able to finish the taco pie, drink two glasses of milk, and still face a dessert of ice cream and gingersnaps. As she put her dishes into the dishwasher, she decided that eating under stress made sense. Fear made people cold. She'd been cold all day. And food, with all those nice calories, made people warm. Eating was a security blanket, much better than the quilt on her bed.

After lunch, she tried the television again. For a while, she watched Tom and Jerry cartoons, and for a while she felt better. But then, as she watched the mice laying another trap for Tom, it struck her. Here it was the middle of the afternoon, when kids were in school, and the cartoons were on. That meant they had to be on so that really little kids—toddlers, preschoolers—would watch. And what were they learning as they watched? That the way to handle someone

24

you didn't like or someone you disagreed with was to drop an anvil on his head. Or put a cannon up his nose. Or cut off his ears. Here was one of the greatest civilizations the world had ever known purposely teaching their littlest kids that weapons were fun. Jeremy was at day care, and she didn't think they watched television at day care. She hoped not. She didn't want to imagine her baby brother, all round cheeks and freckles and big blue-green eyes, learning a Tom and Jerry approach to life. How could their parents let him watch television on Saturday mornings?

She turned off the set again. Television ought to be banned. What good was it, anyway? She went to the dining room to watch the guppies. Watching fish in an aquarium was supposed to be relaxing. In fact, they'd bought the guppies in the first place because her mother wanted to see if they could help her get over the stress of her job. A few of the tiny fish were hovering in the protection of the plastic plants. Some darted occasionally from one side of the tank to the other. They looked fragile. Too fragile. A good hard blow against the glass and the guppies' whole world would be gone. They'd all flow out with the water and flop around on the floor until they died. Wonderful. So much for relaxation.

Whitney got herself another handful of gingersnaps and went into the living room, where she sank onto the couch. The sun shone in the windows and across the rug. The sun, an ongoing nuclear explosion.

"Stop it!" she said out loud. "Do something. Think about something else!" She looked around the room, hoping for a distraction. Bookcases lined both sides of the fireplace. Maybe

25

there was a book there that would take her mind somewhere safe. She used to be able to get right inside a book, especially a mystery, as if she were right there with the main character, doing everything he did, thinking his thoughts, feeling his feelings. People could talk to her then while she was reading, and she wouldn't even hear them. That's what she needed now. A very good, very exciting story.

An hour later, Whitney felt worse. She'd tried reading a Sherlock Holmes and then a Robert Ludlum spy thriller her father always said was the best escapist fiction he knew. But she'd ended up reading the same pages over and over again, unable to make any sense of the words. They just seemed to go in her eyes and out the top of her head without connecting anywhere. She'd scanned all the rest of the titles on the shelves, but hadn't found any that seemed any more promising. By the time she'd gotten to the bottom where the reference books were, she'd given up hope. There was the whole encyclopedia and all she could think of was what a waste it had been for all those people to work so hard to accumulate all the knowledge in those pages, when people were about to die out.

She was sitting in the corner of the couch, just glaring at the sunlight, when the doorbell rang. Gratefully, she got up to answer it.

"Mission of Mercy calling, ma'am. We've received word that someone in this household is traumatized, distraught, and suffering from twentieth century-itis." Paul stood on the front porch. His expression was earnest under his long, raggedly-cut hair. As always, he wore a dirty sweat shirt, scruffy blue jeans, and threadbare sneakers.

26

"You've been talking to Allie," she said, and held the door open for him. "Am I glad to see you. Come on in."

He shook his head. "The inside of a house is no place to be on a day like today. You need sunshine and fresh air."

"While there's still some left?"

"Or while we're still here to notice. Allie couldn't come. She was going to the library or something."

"So she sent you in her place. She hasn't the nerve to talk to me—or listen to me."

Paul shook his head. "I don't want to offend you, Whit, but I don't think it has anything to do with you. I got the definite impression she was meeting someone at the library. It isn't you and it isn't me—which leads me to believe there could be some romantic aspect to this meeting."

"She didn't mention it this morning."

"Many things can happen in six hours. Many things, in fact, can happen during lunch hour. I won't mention the first that comes to mind. You want to walk?"

Whitney looked up at the clear blue sky, crisscrossed by a pair of jet contrails, and nodded. "I guess so. It can't be worse than sitting around inside. This has been the most grotesque day of my life." She sniffed. It was the kind of spring afternoon that used to make her rush home from school to put on roller skates. Then she and Allie would spend the rest of the afternoon, until they were called in for supper, circling the neighborhood. It was the smell that reminded her of that time most, she thought—a kind of damp but fresh, brisk smell. It was the way sunlight ought to smell when it came out in the rain and produced rainbows.

Paul shrugged off his backpack and set it on the porch

swing. It was an army surplus pack that looked as if it had been through a world war—or two. It bulged with books. "That thing weighs three tons. Okay if I leave it here?"

"Sure, if you think it's safe."

"Who would steal textbooks? You couldn't even give them away on a street corner." Paul started down the porch stairs, then turned back. "You coming?"

"Just a minute. Would you like a granola bar?"

"You got pickles? I'd rather have a pickle."

"Sometimes I think you must take lessons in Weird."

"Don't need to. It's in the genes. Dill, please."

Whitney got herself two granola bars, put one in her pocket, and opened the other. She took the largest dill pickle in the jar and went back outside. "Here. Where are we going?"

"How about the Old Place. We haven't been there in a long time."

"Are you sure it's still there? The big house has been bought again. Probably for offices. Won't they have torn it down?"

"It's still there. I went by last weekend, and it doesn't look much worse than it ever did. They'll probably leave it alone until they need more parking space. Then they'll bulldoze the whole estate, gardens and all."

Paul had found the Old Place years before, and he and Whitney and Allie had often played there. It was a gazebo, a garden summerhouse, its upper half built of latticework, with a slate roof that matched the house and carriage house of the estate it belonged to. Set far back on the grounds, where the trees were thickest, it had been ignored over the

28

years and had quietly disintegrated, until, when Paul had discovered it, pieces of the lattice had crumbled away, and many of the slates had fallen from the roof. In places the trees and sky could be seen through the holes overhead. When the big house had changed hands over the years no one had bothered with the gazebo, or with the rose garden that had once surrounded it and was now little more than a tangle of thorns and creepers. It had always been a great place to play, hidden by the overgrown garden and huge oak trees both from the street and from the house. Over the years it had been clubhouse, castle, spaceship, or just a place to go where no one could find them. Whitney hadn't been there for more than a year. For some reason, it seemed exactly the right place to go today.

"Okay, let's go."

For a while they walked without talking, Whitney eating her granola bar, Paul brandishing his pickle as if it were a Groucho Marx cigar. Every so often he would twitch his eyebrows and rush ahead a few steps in Groucho's half-crouching walk. Then he would wait for her to catch up and walk normally for a while. He was trying to get her to laugh, Whitney knew, but it wasn't working. She just didn't feel like laughing.

"So," he said finally. "Allie says this time it's nuclear war."

Whitney nodded.

"Why now? I mean, Hiroshima was in 1945, no?"

"Because I read this book." She told him about *The Fate of the Earth* and what reading it had done to her.

"Grim. Does he think we *have* to have a nuclear war?"

Whitney shrugged. "He doesn't offer much hope for avoiding it. All day I've felt like a character in a catastrophe book. Living the last little bit of my life before it's all over."

Paul didn't laugh or tell her she was crazy or shrug it off. He just walked along, crunching his pickle. When it was gone, he shoved his hands deep into his jeans pockets. "What you need is a Pan Galactic Gargle Blaster."

"A what?"

"It's a fictional drink. Never mind. Tell me more."

Whitney told him how she'd felt that someone in another universe was reading the story of the end of the planet. He stopped in the middle of the sidewalk and looked at her.

"What made you think of that?"

"I don't know, I just did. Like when I read all those disaster books. It was as if while I read, the people who were in the books might really be living through the disasters—and while this other person—I thought of her as a girl, only bigger or something—while she read, I'd be living through mine."

"Hmmmm. You know, Whitney, it could be."

"What? It could be that someone is reading about us right now? Someone in another universe?"

"Sure."

Whitney walked on, leaving him behind. "You're nuts."

He hurried after her. "No I'm not. Sometimes something that occurs to us without any logical explanation is really true. Intuition."

"Well, I don't believe in other universes."

"Big deal. People didn't used to believe in atoms, either. Just because they couldn't see them. The stuff that gets into our mind doesn't have to come from inside, you know—from our senses or our thinking or anything. We get input from outside, too."

"Do you mean like ESP?"

"Something like that. So, maybe there's really another universe—lots of them, maybe. And maybe some of the life forms in those other universes are aware of us the way we're aware of—say an ant colony. One of them *could* write a book about the end of the earth and then someone else could read it. I love it!"

"But how could anyone write about the end of our world if it hasn't happened yet? And how could anyone else be reading about it now? Beforehand. It doesn't make sense."

"Maybe not our kind of sense, Whit, but we're awfully limited, you know. If that person—or life form—who's reading that book is in a different universe, it could be one that's on a different time continuum. Theirs could be going backward from our point of view, so what's future for us would be past for them. Time isn't really a straight line, you know. Einstein proved that."

"Don't talk to me about Einstein. I wouldn't understand it in the first place, and in the second place, if it hadn't been for him, we wouldn't have nuclear weapons now and the whole subject wouldn't have come up."

"Don't knock Einstein—he was a scientist, not a soldier. Anyway, he warned against nuclear war."

"Yeah, well, a lot of good that did. That's like Pandora being sorry after she opened that box and let all the nasties out."

They had reached the iron fence surrounding the estate grounds. A few yards from the corner a huge forsythia bush,

31

growing just inside sprayed its branches over the fence, providing a screen. Just now the screen was partly green with new leaves and partly yellow with the last remnants of blossoms. Paul pulled back a few branches and Whitney slipped in underneath. Long ago Paul had broken out one of the rusty fence rails so they could squeeze through. The fence was broken in other places, and they could easily have gotten onto the grounds elsewhere, but they'd liked the feeling of secrecy their entrance under the bush provided.

It was harder to squeeze through than Whitney remembered. Probably she was getting too big for this. Her mother would blame her fondness for Twinkies and ice cream. Whitney preferred to think she was growing beyond this childish nonsense of sneaking through fences. Anyway, probably no one would bother them, even if they just walked down the driveway and back into the grounds.

The gazebo hadn't changed much. The holes in the roof were probably a bit bigger and there were more tiles littering the ground, but the basic structure seemed about the same. The large rock they had found in the garden and wrestled through the doorway for a chair was still there, streaked with bird droppings. The two peach crates they had brought for supplementary seating had turned gray. Nails protruded oddly where the wood had warped. Whitney brushed at one with her hand and sat down on it gingerly. It held her. Paul perched on the rock and looked up at the roof.

"Doesn't look much worse than it used to. I don't even think anyone else has been here. I used to think we'd come sometime and find vandals had torn it up, or some tramp was using it for a shelter or something."

"Some shelter."

Paul shrugged. "It would be better than the streets."

"I don't think Martinsville has any street people."

"I guess not."

For a while they just sat, taking in the peace and solitude. Except for a few birds and the sound of traffic from the street, it was quiet in the Old Place.

"I really think there might be other universes," Paul said at last.

"It wouldn't matter," Whitney said, kicking a bit of broken slate aside. "Because we'd never know it. And when we blow everything up, what difference will it make anyway? We'll be gone. Even if there are other universes, there wouldn't be human beings there. Maybe a bunch of weird Star Wars creatures."

"But they'd be alive."

Whitney rested her chin on her knee and stared at the stone floor. "No one in any other universe would understand why humans used to go to all the trouble of building things like this place, just to have parties in the garden. Probably no one would understand gardens." She sighed. "Anyway, I don't think there is anyone out there. When we're gone no one will ever know there were roses."

Paul, too, sat quietly, gazing out through the latticework at the garden tangle that was putting out the first leaves of spring. The silence seemed to grow deeper around them. Suddenly they both looked up. There was a strange sound outside the gazebo—a kind of shuffling, dragging sound. It wasn't loud enough to mean there was a person coming. But what animal would make that kind of sound? Not a squirrel,

Whitney thought, or a rabbit, or a pigeon. They listened as the sound came closer and closer. It seemed to be coming directly toward the doorway. It stopped for a moment, and then around the doorframe peered a small, fantastic head on a shimmering blue neck. Its beak was light, its head the same shimmering blue of the neck, but with a vivid white stripe on either side of its tiny eye. A frill of plumes rose above its head like a crown. The bird stared for a moment at Whitney, then at Paul, as if surprised to see them there. Then it walked gravely past the doorway, its long plume of tail trailing behind it.

Whitney and Paul looked at each other without moving. "Was that what I think it was?" Paul asked.

"Of course it was," Whitney said. "What's a peacock doing here?"

❦ 4 ❦

Whitney went to the doorway and stood looking after the peacock. She could still hear it, but it had disappeared behind a knot of rosebush and creeper between the trunks of two large trees. She would have gone after it, but didn't want to frighten it away. Perhaps if they stayed quiet, it would come back. Paul joined her at the doorway, and she put her finger to her lips to stop him from saying anything. After a few minutes, though, the sound had faded. Apparently, the peacock wasn't coming back. "Do you believe that?" she asked. "A peacock?"

"Maybe it escaped from a zoo."

"Do they 'escape'? Don't they just stay wherever somebody feeds them? I thought they were sort of like extra fancy chickens—domesticated like that, anyway. I mean, they aren't wild."

Paul shrugged. "I think they're wild in India or someplace, not in Pennsylvania. Where's there a zoo around here, anyway? I'll bet the nearest one's Philadelphia."

Whitney shrugged. "Maybe there's one of those little animal farms somewhere near. Out in the country. You know, where they keep a couple of raccoons and a fox and a deer

35

and get tourists to pay to see them. Maybe it got away from one of those."

"Could be, I guess. Do peacocks fly?"

"Well, they're birds."

"So are ostriches. I don't think I've ever seen a peacock flying."

"They must. I saw one on the roof of a zoo building once. How would he get up there if he didn't fly?"

"Yeah, but maybe they fly like chickens. Only a little way and not very well. If that's all he could fly, he can't have come very far. I can't see a peacock walking thirty miles into town from some little zoo in the country."

Whitney hugged herself. The sun was beginning to slip down toward the treetops and the warm spring air was taking on the beginning of an evening chill. "I hope he'll be okay. It still gets pretty cold at night around here."

"Not much we could do about it anyway, is there?"

Whitney sighed. "I guess not." She turned and looked at Paul. "That's the whole trouble, you know? There isn't much we can do about anything. I hate being a kid."

Paul picked a flake of paint off a bit of broken lattice and dropped it on the floor. "I don't know if it's any better for adults. Suppose you were forty right now. What would you be able to do for that peacock?"

"I don't just mean about the peacock. I mean about everything. Kids are so helpless."

"Well, think about it. Why are we any more helpless than most adults? About the peacock or about bigger things, like war. Imagine you were forty years old right now instead of fourteen. What could you do?"

"If I were president I could do something."

"Oh sure, a forty-year-old female president. But that isn't what I mean. Anybody could say that. 'If I were president I would dismantle all the nuclear weapons and have all the plutonium shot out into space.' I mean for real, Whitney. If you were just an ordinary adult living in this town, going about your daily life, what would you be able to do that you can't do now?"

"Vote."

"Terrific. And what, exactly, does the vote of one person do? You couldn't elect a president or kick one out, let alone take away nuclear weapons, with one vote."

Whitney kicked at the doorframe. The gazebo shuddered slightly. "That's why I wish I hadn't read that book. If there's nothing I can do—or anybody else can do for that matter— what good does it do even to know about it? Except to scare me to death." She looked up through a hole in the roof to the blue sky that was almost imperceptibly darker now. "What if while we were standing here just like this, looking up at the sky, it started. A flash and we'd be gone. Vaporized. Melted. Along with everything in town. It could happen. Right now it could happen. Tomorrow. Next week."

"Don't be silly, Whit. You don't think the Russians are going to target a little town like this? There aren't even any military bases around here. No crucial industries, no missile silos, not even enough population to bother about. They're not going to aim a missile at Martinsville, P.A."

"You just don't know! That's the whole trouble, Paul. I don't think most people know anything about it. They think nobody wants a war. They think nobody's planning a war.

37

Well, people *are* planning one. The Russians are and so are we, no matter how much everybody talks about working for peace. We even have plans to use nuclear weapons first. But who goes first doesn't even matter anymore. There are so many warheads right this minute they could hit all the important targets and all the little towns like Martinsville, too, and we could do the same thing to them. And both sides are building more every single day."

"Okay, so I don't know all that much about it. But one thing I do know: nobody wants the world to end. What would that prove? Why would anybody want that? Anyway, it hasn't happened yet, so why should it happen now? It's been possible for forty years."

"Not really. Not like now." Whitney went out into the remnants of the rose garden. Shadows were growing longer, and the red-green new leaves of the rosebushes were beginning to look brown in the softening light. She touched a rose branch that was wrapped 'round and 'round with honeysuckle vine. Thorns poked out from the spiral of green vine. "Anyway, I don't say it's going to happen right now. I just say it could. Maybe it won't happen next week, or even next year. Maybe it won't even happen till after this old place has finally been bulldozed away or just falls down on its own. But it'll happen. It's like the ticking on a time bomb. With each tick it doesn't happen, but each tick brings it closer. It's practically certain in our lifetime, probably before we even get a chance to grow up. All those warheads we have already and more being built every day, quicker ones, bigger ones. It'll happen, Paul. Why did we come here, anyway? I'm going home." She began walking toward the fence. She'd wanted to get out of the house when Paul came, but now she wanted to be back in her room on her bed with her comforter pulled over her head.

"Hey, wait up." Paul came along behind her. "So what are you going to do? Hole up in your room like a hermit? What good will that do? What about school? What about your parents? You think you can just quit?"

Whitney trudged ahead without answering. What could she answer, anyway? She didn't know what she was going to do. Paul hadn't helped. If only he'd been able to laugh her out of it. The only thing he'd offered was the same old false hope, "It hasn't happened so far." Well, the gazebo hadn't fallen down so far, either, but nobody'd be dumb enough to bet it would last another hundred years.

When her mother came home from work with Jeremy in tow, Whitney was back in her room, lying on her bed with a teen romance novel, trying to immerse her brain so thoroughly in mindless mush that she couldn't think. It wasn't working. The big question for the girl in the book was whether Lance (that was actually his name!) would kiss her or not. "There won't be a world left to get married in," she wanted to say to this violet-eyed, blond nitwit.

Jeremy pushed open her door and rushed in to throw himself on her. "Giddy-up horse," he said, clambering onto her back and bouncing on her rear.

"Uumph—Jere, get off! You're breaking my back!"

Marianne Whitehurst stuck her head around Whitney's door. "Stay away from Whitney, Jeremy! We don't want you to get her flu! Come back here."

39

"She won't give me any flu, will you, Whit? Will you?"

Whitney dropped her book and rolled over, wrestling Jeremy to her bed and tickling him. "No, little boy, I won't give you any flu. I like you *too* much! Too tickly much!"

"No, no, no," Jeremy squealed. "Let me up!"

"Whitney!"

"It's okay, Mom," Whitney said, and patted her brother on the head. "I'm not going to tickle him to death."

"Are too!" Jeremy wriggled away and stood up. "Look at my shirt, Whitney. Mom says I'm wearing my lunch. Can you see my baloney samwich?"

"All I see is the mustard. It's turned half your shirt yellow!"

"Like a finger painting! That's a mustard sun."

"Whitney, are you feeling better now?" their mother asked. "Are you going to be able to eat dinner with the rest of us, or do you want some soup and crackers up here?"

Soup and crackers for dinner? Whitney was cold again, and starving. "I think I could manage real food now. What're we having?"

"I'm thawing some chicken. I was going to barbecue it, but if you think your stomach would handle it better, I could microwave it with onion soup mix instead."

"That'd be great, Mom. With mashed potatoes. And frozen peas. You want some help?"

"No thanks. Kate should be home any time. I'd rather you stay here and rest. I want you well enough to go back to school tomorrow. Come on now, Jeremy. Leave your sister alone and let her get some more rest. Come watch the 'Electric Company.'"

"Do I have to?"

"Yes, you have to." And they were gone, leaving Whitney in the dim silence of her room.

Back to school. Whitney wished she didn't have to face that. But after today, she knew it wasn't any better to hang around an empty house. At least at school she might be able to think about something else. At least there were other people. Trouble is, there would also be plenty to remind her of the end of the world. If she could be reminded of it reading a romance novel, what was safe? What would happen when someone suggested it was important to learn the names of the principal rivers in China? Learn them while there was still a China? While there were still rivers? While there was still a brain inside her skull that could learn? Maybe, though, it would be better than watching guppies.

Kate was driving Whitney crazy. She insisted on using a knife and fork when she ate chicken, and that made everybody else look like some kind of pig. Prim little picky bits of chicken she'd manage to get off a bone, and then she'd put them in her mouth and nibble away—like a rabbit. Teeny little nibbles. Sometimes it seemed as if Kate purposely ate the way she thought a poet ought to eat, not like a normal human being. As if she ate for an audience. Whitney always used a fork at first, but when she got down toward the bone, a fork was just a waste. Even her mother and father chewed the meat off the bones. Jeremy, with no need to impress anyone, held his drumstick in both hands and gnawed it right from the start. Like a dog. And when he got a bit of something he couldn't chew, he'd just spit it out on the plate. Maybe not really appetizing to watch, but a lot more honest.

Why was that bothering her, anyway, Whitney wondered. Such a little thing, really. Better to have an alive, pain-in-the-neck sister, than one dead of radiation poisoning. Better to have chicken to eat—any old way—than to starve. People are too concerned with petty things, Whitney decided. Herself included. Why don't they think about important issues?

The conversation at dinner tonight had not been deeply interesting. Jeremy had gone on about a fight in the day-care playground until he'd been told to stop talking and eat; Kate had announced that Gordon had tickets to a rock concert Friday night, and there was an argument about whether she'd be allowed to go. Their father had said absolutely not, their mother had interceded.

"They'll destroy their eardrums," William Whitehurst said. "No daughter of mine is going to go through life saying 'Eh, what?' every other minute because she went through an adolescent conformity stage at sixteen."

"She could wear earplugs," Marianne Whitehurst suggested.

"*Mother!*" Kate had protested. "I couldn't. You're kidding, right?"

"Yes."

"Well I'm not," their father had said. "That's not a bad idea."

"Dad!"

"Do you want to go?" he'd asked, waving a fork full of mashed potatoes in the air.

"Of course I want to go!"

"Then wear earplugs. They'd cut down the decibels to a safe range. Loud as those concerts are, you'll still hear plenty."

"Dad!"

During the conversation, Whitney had been trying to decide whether to mention the subject of nuclear war. She'd decided it would be better for them to know the truth about the world, and then she'd decide it would be better not to. She wished she didn't know, after all. Why should she put that burden on them? And maybe it would be better to tell them when Jeremy wasn't around. He was too little to understand. She didn't want to scare him. What if she told them and they didn't believe her? Or what if they believed her and dismissed it the way Paul had? What if they made fun of her? That was the worst possibility of all.

"Well, Whitney?"

She looked up. Her father was looking at her, waiting for some kind of answer. What had she missed?

"I asked if you were feeling better."

Whitney nodded.

"You've hardly said a word tonight. Are you sure you're all right?" Her mother's eyebrows were drawn tight over her eyes in that worried-mother look that drove Whitney crazy. It made her feel somehow guilty—as if anything that might be bothering Whitney was making her mother miserable. That was the worst part of having a mother with a high-pressure job. Nobody at home dared add to the pressure.

She wanted to say she was all right. But she didn't want to say that either, because she wasn't all right. She wasn't going to get to grow up and have a family of her own to sit at the dinner table arguing about rock concerts or worrying about the daughter who wasn't speaking. To Whitney's horror, she felt her eyes brimming with tears. Quickly, she looked down into her lap, where her napkin lay, twisted into a tight roll. When had she done that? If only the tears didn't spill over—if only no one would notice. Then she wouldn't have to explain.

"Whitney's crying!" Jeremy said. "Look, Mommy, Whitney's crying."

Whitney felt the tears making a warm trail down each cheek. Now she would have to tell them. And they would laugh. They would tell her she was making a mountain out of a molehill. Her father said that a lot. They would say it was another one of her silly terrors.

It wasn't silly. It wasn't.

She pushed back her chair and ran up the stairs to her room, her feet sounding like sledgehammers as she went. She slammed her door and threw herself face down onto her bed.

❦ 5 ❦

Whitney's head was full of images she couldn't shut out.
There were pictures she remembered from a movie, of missiles streaking across a clear blue sky, leaving clouds of white
vapor behind them. In the movie people had stood watching
them, shielding their eyes with one hand, not really understanding what it meant, not really understanding that after
these missiles had gone others would come, bringing the
blinding flashes of light, the heat of a star, the fire, the wind,
the rain of radiation. They had stood watching as if they
were watching jets, leaving their trails across the sky, not
knowing that they were watching the countdown to the end
of the human race, the end of the earth.

Over and through the images flooded an overpowering
sense of loneliness. Loneliness for herself, as if she were the
only person in the world to see these visions, to feel so afraid,
and loneliness for the earth, like a little blue ball floating
through the silent, cold darkness of space, with no eyes to
see it happening, no mind to feel sorry, no heart to mourn all
the birds and animals and plants and stupid humans.

What did it matter that there had been people for thousands, maybe millions of years? In the cold, empty universe,
that was no time at all. Less than the blink of an eye.

"The blink of an eye." Whitney shuddered at the expression. It was a way of measuring time in the scale of human life. But after the bombs there would be no more eye blinks, no more people to break time into pieces, no minds to conceive of time. There would forever be nothing but lifeless bits of rock circling suns, suns burning themselves out, black holes sucking up light.

Whitney pressed her fists into her eyes trying to escape the mental pictures, but they kept coming. Planets circling suns, black spaces pricked with light, sprays of galaxies. A universe empty of life. Empty even of the knowledge that life had been.

She rolled from side to side, feeling as she moved her own, single, tiny, helpless life and wanting somehow to believe it was stronger than death, that it would go on and on in spite of everything.

There was a knock at the door. She stopped moving. They'd think she was crazy, crying first and then thrashing on her bed like this. They'd think she was possessed or crazy. Nobody would understand the fear that had eaten its way into her brain and her muscles and her bones. The knock came again, but she lay very still and said nothing, her fists still pressed to her eyes.

"Whitney? What is it? What's the matter?" Her mother came into the room. Whitney heard the door, heard the footsteps and her mother's voice getting closer. Still, she didn't move. "Whitney, won't you talk to me? Are you still sick?"

A hand touched her shoulder. Whitney brought her knees to her chin, hunching herself into a ball, and said nothing.

46

"Honey, please talk to me. Is it something someone said at dinner? Is it Allie? Have you had another fight with Allie? Or Paul? Has something happened at school?"

She could hear the concern in her mother's voice, feel it in the hand on her shoulder. But what good was it? What could her mother say that would make any difference? Whitney wished she were Jeremy's age again. She wished she could climb into her mother's lap to be cuddled. She wished she could go back to when cuddling was enough, when she could believe that her mother and father could do anything. As if they were as powerful as God, and their arms around her made her safe from anything bad. She wanted her mother to hold her and tell her that there would never be a nuclear war. Never. Not by accident and not because someone purposely pushed a button. And she wanted to be able to believe it. But it couldn't be. The safe time was gone forever, and Whitney knew it.

She wanted to talk about it. She did. She could even feel the words forming in her mouth. But they wouldn't come out. She was afraid that if she said anything, her mother would dismiss her fear. She didn't want to hear that voice tell her it was foolish to be afraid of a nuclear war—as if it were a nightmare she'd had about a monster in the closet. She didn't want to hear that getting her rest and going back to school were more important than the future of the human race. Those were the things her mother would say. Whatever the actual words would be, that's what they would mean. "Don't be silly," she would say. "You've just gotten yourself all worked up over nothing, the way you always do. Nothing's ever as bad as you think it is. Just get your sleep and every-

47

thing will be all right in the morning. Everything always looks better in the morning, see if it doesn't."

How, Whitney wondered, could she survive hearing her mother say those things? She stayed as she was, curled in that tight little ball, and said nothing.

There was a long silence while her mother tried to decide what to do. Whitney fought down the urge to turn over and throw herself into her mother's arms. Not even the hardest, longest hug in the world could take away this fear.

"All right, lovey. Maybe you'll feel like talking tomorrow." The warm hand moved to her forehead. "You don't seem to have a fever. Things always look worse at night. I'm sure you'll feel better in the morning."

So there were the words anyway. At least her mother didn't know what it was she was dismissing. She didn't know that morning could only make this fear worse, could only bring the end a few hours closer. Whitney held very still and waited. Finally, with a sigh, her mother turned away. There was a pause by the door, and she knew her mother was standing there, looking at her, frowning and worrying, but she didn't move a muscle. At last the door closed and she heard the click as it latched.

Slowly, she got up, then took off her clothes and put her pajamas on. She was cold again, but this time it was a deep, inside cold. It was too early to go to sleep; she wasn't tired. Maybe she could read for a while. What, though? *The Fate of the Earth* still lay on top of her schoolbooks, and she avoided looking at it. She picked up the romance novel again. Allie loved these; there had to be something to them. Maybe she could get interested in Lance, if she tried hard enough.

Maybe she could push away the images of catastrophe with images of young love. Maybe.

When her alarm woke Whitney the next morning, it interrupted a dream again. She couldn't remember what the dream had been about, exactly, only that the peacock had been in it. She remembered that brilliant blue head with the white stripes above and below the eyes, and that little white feathered crown. Had she seen the rest of him? She only remembered the head, the bright eyes looking at her, and behind them the deep greenery of a forest—not the garden at the Old Place, but a deep, vibrant green jungle.

Gray light filtered into her room, and she became aware of the sound of rain against the window. Good. An ugly day. Maybe she could face going out today, if only she could keep herself from thinking and remembering. She stretched and sat up. She wasn't so cold this morning. Instead, she felt numb. Quiet and numb inside. It felt better.

Just as she finished dressing and was about to head for the bathroom to brush her teeth, Jeremy burst into her room, his hair sticking up all over his head, as it usually did in the morning before anyone had attacked it with hairbrush and water.

"You all well, Whitney?" he asked, as he crashed into her legs. "You going to school today?"

She reached down and picked him up, breathing in the little-boy smell of him. "Yes, I am," she said, and tried to smooth his hair down. It sprang right back up under her hand. "Why do you want to know?"

" 'Cause if you were sick and had to stay home, I was

49

gonna be sick, too, and stay home with you. We could build a whole city with my blocks and make up a story about it. That's the mostest fun we ever have, but you never have time. Stay home, please!"

Whitney hugged him hard and then put him down. "You remind me when you get home tonight, and we'll build a city before dinner. I promise."

"All *right!*" he yelled, and ran for the door. He went out into the hall, then stuck his head back in. "You promise? For sure and cross your heart and hope to die?"

Whitney shivered. "Promise. Hope to die." She shoved *The Fate of the Earth* off her schoolbooks and loaded them into her backpack, repeating the title of each textbook as she picked it up. It was going to take an effort all day to keep her mind occupied. Where did "cross your heart and hope to die" come from, anyway?

In the kitchen, Marianne Whitehurst was checking the contents of her briefcase and trying to drink her coffee at the same time. When Whitney came in, she looked up, a frown creasing her forehead. Whitney thought, as she did every morning, how nice her mother looked before she went off to work—so crisp and professional. Even in the middle of the morning rush, when she was trying to get Jeremy to finish his cereal or looking for her car keys, she looked capable. Whitney could almost believe her mother could fix everything when she looked like that.

"Well? You feeling better?"

Whitney managed a smile. "Just like you said—everything looks better in the morning."

Her mother made a face and glanced out the window over

50

the sink. "You think that looks better, do you? And I can't find my umbrella."

"Use mine," Kate said, coming into the kitchen with her books and jacket. "Gordon's driving today, so I won't need it."

"Great. Is your father up, or did he go back to sleep? Today's his early class."

"He's up," Whitney said. "I heard him singing in the bathroom."

"Singing! Well, I'm glad everyone else seems to like days like this. You sure you're well enough to go to school today, Whit?"

"I'm sure."

"Have your father write a note for you—stomach flu. Don't forget now." Whitney shook her head. "Come on, Jeremy, we'll be late. I never know how the car will act in the rain."

When they'd gone, Whitney tore the top off a packet of instant oatmeal and poured it into a bowl. Kate was putting together her morning health drink of instant milk and protein powder and brewer's yeast. Maybe she would understand, Whitney thought. "Kate, have you ever read *The Fate of the Earth*?"

Kate turned on the blender. The mixture swirled up and turned slightly brown, white foam forming on the top. When she'd turned it off, Kate made a face. "You mean that awful thing about nuclear war?" Whitney nodded. "I started it, but I quit. Too gruesome."

"Didn't you want to find out what he had to say about it?"

Kate shook her head. "Are you kidding? Nobody who starts a book out that way is going to give any neat answers. I'd rather have neat answers. And if there aren't any, which

51

seems to be the point, I'd rather not think about it. You know? Why would anybody want to think about it? That's just paranoid." She poured her drink into a glass, took a deep breath, and gulped it down. "Oh, yuck, I hate that stuff!"

"Then why do you drink it?"

"It's supposed to be very good for you. You should have it, too, you know. It isn't even all that bad if you put banana in it. But Mom keeps forgetting to buy bananas." Kate took an apple out of the bowl next to the refrigerator and gathered her books. "Gordon'll be here any minute. Don't read that book, Whitney. You don't want to know how many weeks it takes to die of radiation sickness. Really."

Whitney sighed. Too late. Why hadn't Kate told her that last week? "See you later," she said.

"Right." And Kate headed for the living room to watch for Gordon, leaving Whitney alone with her bowl of maple and brown sugar oatmeal and the sound of the rain.

❦ 6 ❦

"It's the only thing to do, Whitney," Paul said, leaning toward her so she could hear him over the noise in the lunchroom. "You should see yourself. You look like a zombie. Or like those cartoon guys with the signs that say 'The End Is at Hand' or something."

Whitney took a bite of her peanut butter and jelly sandwich and chewed it up before answering. "It is."

"Well, not today, it isn't. I don't blame Allie for not wanting to eat with you. I almost ate with some of my many buddies myself. I'm telling you, you've got to join one of those peace groups. Take petitions around. Go on marches. Whatever they do. Write congressmen. Write the president. You have to *do* something. It'll make you feel better. It will."

Whitney sighed. "It won't make me feel better. What good do those groups do? You're the one who said we're all helpless, even the adults who can vote. You're the one who said one vote doesn't count, one vote can't make any change."

"Okay, I did say that. One vote *can't* do anything. But that's the point of the groups. They represent lots of votes. If enough people get together, they can do something. At the very least they can get people to notice them. They can get people to learn and think about it. You said people don't know enough. Well, groups can help teach them. In the last election all the candidates had to take a stand against nuclear war, even the ones who didn't come out for a freeze. Everybody *had* to be against nuclear weapons, one way or another. That wouldn't have happened if those groups hadn't been making such a fuss. Remember in Europe? They made a human chain seventy-five miles long or something like that to protest our missiles being put in Germany."

"Sure. I remember that. And we went right ahead and put our missiles there, didn't we? And it doesn't matter what the candidates say when they're trying to get elected. We go right on making more and more nuclear weapons and talking to the Russians the way little kids talk just before they start slugging each other on the playground."

Paul finished the salami sandwich that was his customary lunch and wiped a spot of mustard from his mouth. The noise in the lunchroom was beginning to die down as people finished eating and left. It was no longer raining, and most people were heading outside. "It's just talk. They're not going to go pushing any buttons."

Whitney had finished her sandwich and looked now at the two chocolate-covered graham crackers she'd brought for dessert. She wished she'd brought more. "Jonathan Schell says that Russia and America are like two guys facing each other with their guns drawn. Neither one wants to shoot first, but each is afraid the other will. So one shoots in self-defense, and so does the other, and they're both dead. And that's the end of the human race."

A tall, dark-haired boy got up from the table next to them and walked past Paul, bumping into him as he went. "Oh, sorry, Einstein." He took a handful of Paul's hair and gave it a sharp tug. "Don't you think it's time for a haircut?"

Another boy laughed. "That's a nice sweat shirt. Cool."

Paul ignored them. With elaborate care, he put his apple core and his plastic sandwich bag into his lunch bag and then folded it all into a neat bundle.

"Come on, Kevin," the second boy called. "He's not worth the time it takes to notice him. Or that fat girl with him, either."

Whitney looked up and made a face, crossing her eyes and baring her teeth.

"Look out, the wild animals are loose!" the boy named Kevin shouted. The people who were left at the nearby tables all turned to stare, and Whitney made the same face at them.

"Don't," Paul whispered, "just ignore them."

"I hate that," Whitney said, and put one of the graham crackers into her mouth. She chewed and swallowed, thinking it didn't taste as good as usual. "Maybe we'd be better off extinct. People are such pigs sometimes."

Paul grinned. "Most of the time, if my experience is any measure. Just try to remember they can't help it. It's bad genes."

Whitney smiled for the first time all day. "Maybe nuclear holocaust is only God's way of trying to tell us something."

"Listen, some people really think that. I heard some fundamentalist preacher saying that God would destroy the world by the fire of nuclear war next time. Of course all the people he was preaching to didn't have to worry about it because they were sure they were all going to survive."

"On earth?"

55

"No, no. They're going to heaven, just as soon as it happens."

"I think I'd rather believe I was going to heaven than be so scared. Wouldn't you?"

"I don't know about that heaven business, Whitney. I mean, where is it? All those radio telescopes we've got trained on the skies and nobody's caught a single glimpse of a golden street. Or even an angel wing. Maybe we'll all get beamed up to another universe, though. Maybe that I could believe."

"Do you believe in God?"

"I don't know. I mean, it isn't that I don't, only that I think we've got Him all wrong. We've oversimplified Him or something. And I really don't think He only cares about our one little planet. I can't see Him putting an end to the earth because we've been naughty. I can sooner imagine a Vogon space ship vaporizing us to make way for a hyperspatial express route."

"What?"

"You know—*Hitchhiker's Guide to the Galaxy*, Whit. I've been trying to get you to read it all year."

"Jonathan Schell says . . ."

Paul stood up and wiped his hands on his scruffy jeans. "If you quote Schell to me one more time today, I'll scream. And then you know what'll happen—we'll be stared at. We could end up unpopular!"

"How awful," Whitney said. She ate her last graham cracker and crumpled her trash into a ball. "Think quick!" she said and tossed it at him. Paul raised one hand, but missed. "That's the whole trouble with you. You can't catch. Between that and being smart, it's no wonder you aren't making it in junior high."

The bell rang to end lunch period and Paul picked up his backpack. "See you later, Whit. I still think you should join a freeze group or something. Think about it, okay?"

Whitney shrugged. "Okay." Paul hurried off. His first class after lunch was science, and he liked to be early.

As Whitney left the lunchroom, she caught a glimpse of Allie, leaning against a window near the front door of the school, her books cradled in her arms, talking to a boy, a very tall, very thin boy Whitney had never seen before. So it hadn't been Whitney's mood that had kept Allie from joining them at lunch after all. She wondered who the boy was, and whether he was the reason Allie had gone to the library after school. Allie had picked her up that morning and they had walked to the bus together, but not a word had been said about a very tall, very thin boy.

"So why didn't you tell me about him?" Whitney asked as she watched Allie gather her things from her locker.

"Who?" Allie asked, slipping into her jacket.

"You know darned well who. Mr. Tall. The one you abandoned us for at lunch."

"Oh, him. Come on, Whit, we'll miss the bus. It left early yesterday." She flung one strap of her backpack over her shoulder and hurried off.

Whitney had to run to catch up. "Yes, him. Don't act so innocent. What's going on?"

"Nothing's going on. He's doing a report for social studies

57

on the same thing I'm doing mine on, so we went to the library after school yesterday, that's all."

"He's in your social studies class?"

Allie's determined calm broke then, and she giggled. "No, silly, he's in the ninth grade. He just transferred here this semester."

"How'd you meet him?"

"At lunch yesterday. He heard me telling Paul I was going to do a report on Mao Tse-tung, and he said he was doing the same thing. Of course mine's for the unit on China, and his is for a unit on the second world war." Allie turned then, and grabbed Whitney by both arms. "Did you see him? Isn't he fantastic?"

Fantastic was exaggerating, Whitney thought. "He's tall, anyway."

"He sure is. Honest, Whitney, I feel practically short when I stand near him."

"Short you're not, Allie."

"I know. But with him it doesn't matter."

"Would you mind loosening your hold on my arms? You're cutting off the circulation."

"Sorry."

"Come on, you said yourself we'd miss the bus."

"His name is James. James Brady."

Whitney hurried to the end of the line that was in the process of boarding bus 53. This was what reading romance novels led to, she supposed. And just now, when she needed Allie more than ever before in her life, she had a definite feeling that Allie was not going to be there. Allie was going to be with James Brady.

*   *   *

Whitney stood in the middle of the kitchen, wondering what to do. She'd already had her after-school snack, a glass of milk and a Ho-Ho from the box her mother had hidden behind the canned tomatoes in the pantry. She wanted another Ho-Ho, but there were only two packs left, and her mother would know for sure she'd found them if she had another. She took an apple instead.

Allie had gone to the library again, to do research with James Brady. Whitney doubted that either of them would learn much about Mao Tse-tung. Paul, too, was busy. His mother, a potter with a definite lack of housewifely skills, had asked him to help her clean house. He'd said it would take at least two hours just to unearth the surfaces that needed cleaning.

Whitney looked out the window into the backyard. A cardinal was sitting on the empty bird feeder, pecking at it as if determination could make sunflower seeds appear. Once spring came, Marianne Whitehurst quit feeding the birds, because they could fend for themselves, she said. The rain had stopped and the sun had come out again, weakly, obscured at intervals by patches of cloud. Whitney decided to visit the Old Place again. Maybe she'd see the peacock. She went up to Kate's room and borrowed her old Penn State hooded sweat shirt. Whitney had one of her own, but it was getting small, and nothing made her so conscious of her squat shape as clothes that were tight on her.

As she walked to the Old Place, Whitney was aware of the movement around her. Cars went by on the street, people stood at corners, waiting for traffic lights to change, a bell

59

clanged at the Gulf station as a car pulled up to the pump. Normal things. Normal life. All as fragile as a sand castle when the tide was coming in. She wondered how many people were thinking, as they drove or walked or put their quarters into parking meters, that it could all end. Probably nobody. That's why it could end. Because nobody was afraid. Nobody thought about it. Everybody was like Allie or Kate. Or Paul, who refused to take it seriously even when he did think about it.

Probably people avoided thinking about it in self-defense. Except, of course, that it was a very minor kind of defense— protecting their comfort while risking everything else. Something was needed to shake people up and get them upset enough to do something. Like the mess at Love Canal. Until then nobody got very excited about waste dumps, and now there was a tremendous fuss about cleaning them up. Love Canal and Times Beach. People understood when they saw pictures of deserted houses and heard about kids getting cancer. But you couldn't have a nuclear holocaust just to let people know how serious it was. Maybe if a bomb went off once, on a real American city, that would do it. People could see newspaper pictures of what was left of the place, pictures of charred people and animals, of withered crops and dead cows. That might make them rise up to make sure nuclear weapons were never used again. Otherwise, people would just assume nothing as bad as that could possibly happen. They'd just go along with their daily lives worrying about whatever they worried about—getting their taxes paid or whether they were going to get a divorce or whether their kids were into drugs or whatever, and not a thought for the future of the whole human race.

The ground was soggy underfoot as Whitney crawled through the fence by the forsythia bush. Only a few yellow flowers still clung to the long branches after the rain, and those were brown at the edges. From now on the bush would be green—its display of yellow color just a brief span compared to the whole rest of the year. Bright and then gone, she thought, like people on the third planet from the sun.

Inside the gazebo there were puddles in the depressions of the stone floor. Reddish buds from the trees overhead floated in them. The old gazebo gave little protection from a solid spring rain. Whitney pushed against the door frame and the whole structure moved slightly, creaking a protest. The sitting stone was wet and the crates soaked. Whitney didn't go inside, but stood, looking at the ruined garden, wondering where the peacock might be, whether it lived somewhere near. Above her the trees were just beginning to get their leaves, but the creepers and vines were already vibrantly green, already sending this year's runners up trunks, around rose branches, across anything that gave them a foothold. Or stemhold, Whitney amended. Birds were singing above her. She didn't know what a peacock sounded like, except that it was bound to be loud. She'd read a story once—a fable—about the peacock. Something about paying for its beautiful plumage with an ugly voice. No ugly voices here.

There were other sounds, too, she realized now—hammering and the sound of a power tool of some kind, coming from the big house. The new owners must be remodeling, she

61

thought. Probably soon they'd send the bulldozers out to knock down all the trees and tear up the old garden to make way for a parking lot. If the peacock had picked this garden to live in, he'd lose his new home when they did that. She wondered if they'd really do it, and then decided that they would. Trees and an ancient garden and a ramshackle summer-house had no business value. What counted was someplace for customers to leave their cars, not someplace for peacocks to live. At the first sign of a bulldozer, she vowed, she'd never come back, not even to find out what had happened to the pea-cock. At the first sign of a bulldozer, she'd keep the Old Place in her memory the way it had been all the years they'd played there.

A squirrel jumped from one tree to another, chittering loudly. Another followed, and the two raced 'round and 'round the trunk, first heading down toward the ground, then back up again, shouting at each other the whole time. Whitney wondered if they were playing or fighting. She liked to imagine what they were saying to each other—"You take your mangy hide off my tree and stay away from my store of acorns or I'll take the end of that ugly thing you call a tail right off." The squirrels were making such a racket that she didn't hear anything until the voice spoke directly behind her.

"Do you come here often?"

Whitney spun around, so startled that it took a moment to catch her breath. She found herself looking up into the face of a woman who towered over her. Whitney wasn't tall herself, so any adult seemed tall to her, but this woman had to be over six feet. She was dressed in faded jeans, heavy work shoes, and a plaid flannel shirt, worn open over a dark turtleneck. She was wearing leather work gloves and holding a pair of new-looking pruning shears in one hand. Her dark hair was utterly straight, cut evenly about an inch above her shoulders and heavily streaked with gray at the sides and through the straight bangs that fell across her forehead nearly to her dark brows. The woman's face was lined around the eyes and mouth, and she was wearing no makeup. Her cheekbones were clearly visible, and her jaw was square. Amazon, Whitney thought. She could be an Amazon warrior.

"Do you?" the woman asked, her voice husky and low—a perfect Amazon voice.

Whitney was still stunned, partly from surprise, partly from the look of the woman, who now put one hand possessively on the gazebo. "I—I used to, when I was littler. My friends and I used to play here."

"And now?"

"I just came—just came to see—" Whitney felt like a fool. Here she was, trespassing, and her reason was going to sound ridiculous. Maybe she hadn't even seen the peacock. It seemed unreal now, especially while this woman was looking at her as if she were a thief or something. "Yesterday I was here, and I saw—well, I saw a peacock. I just wanted to come back and see if it was still here."

"Yesterday? You do come often."

"Oh, no. I mean, I hadn't been here for more than a year. I—I just came yesterday to see if the Old Place had changed any." Whitney didn't mention Paul. She didn't want the woman to get the wrong idea about why they'd come there.

"And has it changed?"

63

"No. I mean except that it's fallen apart a little more. And—and the peacock. That had never been here before."

"Maharajah came with me."

"You? Are you working here?"

The woman laughed a short, dry laugh. Her face didn't change, didn't soften, and the eyes still bored into Whitney. "I suppose you could call it work. I bought the place, and I'm trying to see what I can do with all this." She gestured around her at the tangle of creepers. "It was quite a garden, once."

Whitney nodded. "Lots of roses. Aren't you going to bull-doze everything to make a parking lot?"

"No."

"The peacock is yours?"

"Has been for a couple of weeks. Or maybe I'm his. You don't get a commitment from a peacock. He'll eat what you feed him and that's about all."

"I'm sorry about coming here," Whitney said. "I guess I'm trespassing. I didn't know who'd bought it. My friends and I used to come here all the time and nobody seemed to mind. Nobody paid much attention to this part back here."

"That's obvious. I intend to change that."

"I'd better be going. I won't come back."

The woman didn't say anything for a moment. She just stood, looking at the greenery, almost as if she weren't really seeing it, as if her mind were someplace else. She was beautiful, Whitney thought, in spite of the old clothes. But it was a dark, almost painful beauty. An Amazon warrior who had lost many battles, maybe. At last she looked back at Whitney. "Come when you like. I had a place like this when I was

64

young, and it was important to me. I wouldn't want to take it away from you. As for Maharajah—Raj for short—you'll certainly be able to see him, and hear him, for that matter. Just don't expect to make friends with him. Maybe next time you come things will have changed."

"Are you going to fix the gazebo?"

The dark eyes turned toward the gazebo, and the woman sighed. The sound filled Whitney with sadness. Suddenly the gazebo was like a living thing with a terrible illness. "I don't know if this can be fixed. I think I may be too late for it. But maybe I can still do something for the garden."

"That would be great," Whitney said. "I'd like that kind of change. We just thought with offices in the old house, they'd turn this into a parking lot."

"No. And the house won't be offices, either."

Whitney waited for the woman to explain what the house would be, but she didn't. She just stood, one hand on the gazebo, staring into the trees. The sun fell across one side of her face, shadows shifting as the wind moved the leaves overhead. "I'd better be going now," Whitney said. "But I really would like to come back to see the peacock sometime."

"Fine." The woman shrugged her shoulders, as if shifting a burden. "I'm sorry I didn't introduce myself. I'm Theodora Bourke." She held out one large, gloved hand.

"My name's Whitney," Whitney said, taking the offered hand. Her own felt lost in the firm grip. "Whitney White-hurst."

"Pleased to meet you, Whitney. Come anytime."

With that, the woman turned away and walked back toward the house, stepping over patches of undergrowth, weaving her way among the trees. Whitney watched her go, unable to put into words or even clear thought the way she was feeling. It was almost as if she had met someone out of a fable, out of a myth. She was aware of the sound of hammering again, and the high whine of the power tool. Suddenly both sounds were drowned out by a rasping shriek. The peacock, Whitney thought, greeting its Amazon. She turned and started back toward home. For the first time in two days, she was not thinking about nuclear war.

❦ 7 ❦

By the time Whitney got home, her father and Jeremy were there. Jeremy met her at the door. "Where've you been? You promised," he said. "You promised you would build a block city with me!"

William Whitehurst, in his shirt sleeves, his tie loosened, came out of the kitchen. He had a sandwich in one hand and a can of beer in the other. "He thought you'd be here when we got home and he's been having fits. Wouldn't even have a snack with me."

"Snack?" Whitney said. "That's some snack you're having."

"No time for lunch," her father explained. "We had a department meeting. I was about starved."

"You won't have any room for supper."

"I'll manage."

Whitney ruffled Jeremy's hair and he ducked out from under her hand. "You promised!" he said again.

"I know I did, Jere. And we'll go do it—right now. As soon as you've had your snack."

"I'll be in my study," their father said.

"You could build with us," Whitney suggested.

"I'd love to, but I want to finish the chapter I'm on. Next time, huh?"

"Sure." Whitney took Jeremy's hand. "Let's go. I think I might be able to find you some Ho-Hos. Best fuel in the world for city builders."

When they'd finished the box of Ho-Hos, Whitney and Jeremy took the blocks to the living room. The supply of blocks was enormous. Kate had been given a basic set when she turned two, it had been expanded when she turned four, and then Whitney had been given another set two years later. By the time Jeremy had been given a new set of his own, they had enough, altogether, to build a splendid city. They all belonged to Jeremy now, but Whitney could still "help" him build. Nobody had to know how much fun she had doing it. Even Kate usually helped. Whitney was very proud of her city plans. She let Jeremy do the basic square buildings and even a tower or two, but she laid out the system of streets, decided where everything would go, and finally, when everything else had been completed, added her favorite touch, an elaborate bridge across the river she always put through the center of every town. The river was a long strip of blue material she'd cut and sewed together herself.

While they were working, Kate got home and was allowed to add a church on an empty street corner. Their mother arrived a short time later and Jeremy dragged her in to admire their work before she changed clothes and began fixing dinner. "You seem to be feeling a lot better," she said to Whitney. "School go all right today?" Whitney looked up from the parking garage she was building and nodded. "Things okay with Allie?"

"Sure." At least things were okay with Allie and James

Brady. Whitney didn't know what that was going to mean for Allie and her. Apparently her mother thought the problem last night had been about Allie, and it was easier to let her keep thinking that.

They had to stop work to eat dinner, but right afterward they came back to it. Whitney was really having fun. This was the most elaborate city she'd ever planned.

"It needs a wall," Jeremy said, when the buildings were all completed. He was standing back, frowning and biting his lip. "I want it to have a wall—all around it."

Whitney looked into the block box. There weren't enough blocks left to do a wall and her bridge. "It doesn't need a wall, Jere. If we do a wall, we can't do a bridge."

"Don't care! I want a wall."

"Why? We've never had one before."

"It needs a wall to keep the bad peoples out."

"Bad peoples?" Jeremy had never worried about bad people when they were building a city before.

"Bad peoples! This is a city just for good peoples, and I don't want bad ones to get in."

"But the bridge . . ."

Jeremy frowned. "We don't need a bridge."

"But how will people get across the river?"

"They can swim. I want a wall around the whole city. I want it, Whitney!" Jeremy looked as if he were about to cry.

"Okay, okay. I guess we can have a ferry to get people across the river." Whitney was surprised at how disappointed she was about her bridge. It was always her favorite part. Still, she was too old to fight about whether they had a bridge or a wall. How dumb could anyone get? Maybe Jeremy didn't like bridges because she didn't let him help with them. "We'll have a wall. You start on that side, and I'll start on this side."

The wall was boring to build, but it didn't take them long. Whitney made a gate, explaining that the good people had to be able to get out, and then decided on a drawbridge so the bad people couldn't get in. She built two towers to hold the drawbridge, and it turned out to be almost as much fun as the bridge would have been. Finally, they were finished. Jeremy went to get his Fisher-Price people and cars. They were out of scale, but he didn't seem to mind. He always wanted to have people in the cities when they were finished, because he liked to play with them afterward. Usually, with everyone being careful, a block city could last for a week, and he'd play there every evening, making up stories for the people to act out, cheerfully ignoring the fact that the cars took up whole streets and that people standing next to buildings were nearly two stories high.

Together, they positioned the people, with Jeremy giving the orders this time. Marianne Whitehurst came in once to remind them of the time. Kate went out with Gordon, and their father retired to his study again, after admiring the city to Jeremy's satisfaction. Finally, the last person had been placed, the last car parked in front of its house. "All done," Whitney said. "Time for bed."

"Not yet," Jeremy protested. "I amn't finished."

"I'm not. There's no such word as 'amn't.' "

"Gregory says amn't," Jeremy protested.

70

"Well, Gregory's wrong."

"He is not!" Jeremy's face clouded over and his lower lip seemed to grow as he glared at her. "Anyway, I *like* 'amn't!' "

"Okay, okay. You amn't finished. What else do we need?"

Jeremy grinned. "You'll see. Close your eyes."

Whitney obeyed, wondering what he was going to do. It was a wonderful city, she decided. Even without the bridge. The wall gave it a character all its own. And there wasn't a single block left in the box. She couldn't remember the last time they'd used every single block. This city was probably some kind of record. She wondered where Jeremy had gone. She was getting tired of keeping her eyes closed. Finally, she heard him coming back, making the sound of some kind of engine.

"Brrrrrrrr," he droned. "Brrrrrrrrrr. Here comes the airplane. Brrrrrrrrrrr."

Airplane! She'd forgotten he had a new plane. They should have built an airport. Next time she'd have to remember that.

"Brrrrrrr," he said. "You can open your eyes, now, Whitney. The plane's almost there."

She opened her eyes in time to see Jeremy swoop down over the city, his new plane in one hand, and a basketball in the other. "Jeremy!" she shouted. "Don't!" But she was too late. He had already thrown the basketball.

"Boom!" he yelled. "Boom, boom, boom!"

The basketball dropped into the center of the city, knocking down the buildings, then bounced and came down again, taking out Kate's church, a school, part of the wall, and the drawbridge. Toy cars and people were scattered about under

71

the fallen blocks, and Jeremy was circling the city, kicking over the wall as he went, still zooming his plane around and around.

"Bombed it all down," he said. "The plane bombed it all down. Brrrrrrrrrr . . ."

Before she knew what she was doing, Whitney had grabbed Jeremy's arm and dragged him away from the city. Nearly choking on her rage, she snatched the plane out of his hand and threw it down. It skidded across the rug and collided with the wall, breaking off one plastic wing. She held Jeremy's shoulders then, and shook him as hard as she could. "Why did you do that, Jeremy?" she shouted. "Why did you do that? Why, why, why?"

Suddenly, her father was between them, his hands hurting her wrists as he pulled Jeremy free. Jeremy was crying, and her father's face was twisted with fury. "Don't you ever do anything like that again," he said. His voice was terrible. "Don't you ever do that again. Do you hear me, Whitney?"

She nodded. Jeremy had run to their mother, who had come in from the kitchen and was hugging him now, patting his back as he sobbed. She looked at her father again, his face blurring through her tears. What had happened to her? What had she done?

"Shaking a child can cause brain damage, Whitney." Her father's voice hadn't changed. She couldn't remember seeing him this angry. "Go to your room. I don't want to see you again tonight."

Whitney went. When she'd closed her door, she sat on the edge of her bed and began to sob. What had happened? Could she really have caused Jeremy brain damage? Just from

72

shaking him? She hadn't meant to hurt him. She didn't know what she'd meant to do. She hadn't even had time to think about it. One minute Jeremy was throwing that basketball at their city, the next she was yelling and shaking him. Why had she done that? It was only a stupid block city. Why had she been so angry? She grabbed her pillow and cradled it in her lap, as if it could offer her comfort. She rocked back and forth, her face in the pillow. She wished now that she were dead. It would be better to be dead than to do terrible things to Jeremy, better to be dead than to live the way she had for the last two days.

At first Whitney ignored the knock on her door. She didn't want to talk to anyone. Especially her father. What would he do to her? The knocking came again.

"Whitney, I'm coming in."

It *was* her father. The door opened and she heard him coming over to her. She kept her face in her pillow, pushed into it so hard she could hardly breathe. Suddenly the pillow was gone. Her father had jerked it away. She felt exposed, defenseless. She half expected him to hit her.

"I want an explanation. Look at me, Whitney."

Whitney did as she was told. She was afraid not to. She could feel her heart beating inside her chest as if it might pound a hole through her ribs. He was standing over her bed, his fists on his hips, his eyes blazing. Whitney looked away from him, staring instead at the yellow rug at his feet, at the toes of his shoes, and wiped the tears from her cheeks with the back of her hand.

"I want an explanation for your behavior."

"I . . . don't . . ." she started. What could she say? "I don't have an explanation. I don't know why I did it."

"Are you telling me it was an unprovoked attack on a four-year-old?"

"Not exactly. I just . . . I just mean that I don't really know why I reacted the way I did." Whitney felt tears sliding down her cheeks again. She sniffed, wishing she could blow her nose.

"Jeremy did something to you?"

"Yes. No. I mean, he did something, but not to me, really."

"What?"

"He knocked our city down." The moment she'd said it, she understood how it sounded. But it was too late. Her father looked as if he were about to explode.

"A fourteen-year-old attacks her baby brother for knocking down her block city?"

"It wasn't just that, Daddy. Honest it wasn't. He was bombing it. He was playing he was a plane and he was bombing the city down!"

William Whitehurst made a visible effort to control himself. Very carefully, he lowered his arms. "There is a difference?"

And then she was crying again, trying to get words out, but unable to make a single, sensible sentence. "He's too . . . he shouldn't . . . what does he know about . . ." She buried her face in her hands and felt the tears leaking out between her fingers. What did she mean to say? How could she make her father understand when she didn't understand herself?

After a moment she felt her father's hands on her upper

arms, holding her firmly. "Stop it now, Whitney. Get hold of yourself. You aren't making sense."

She sniffed again and took a long, deep breath. When she looked up, he had knelt beside her bed. He was still angry, but didn't seem so frightening now that his eyes were on a level with her own. The sniffing had done no good. Her nose was dripping. He noticed, took a tissue from the box on her bedside table, and handed it to her. She nodded her thanks and blew her nose. Then she swabbed at her face with the wadded tissue and clutched the damp lump as if it could give her courage. "There's going to be a war," she said at last.

Her father sat back on his heels. "What? What has that to do with anything?"

"There's going to be a nuclear war. And the human race will be extinct. Jeremy's already bombing cities, and he's only four. And he doesn't even watch a lot of violent television. Think how other little kids must be!"

"Let me get this right. Are you telling me that you went after Jeremy because he bombed your city and that made you afraid there would be a war?"

"I was already afraid of that," Whitney said, sniffing again. "There *will* be a war, and that will be the end of everything. Jonathan Schell says so."

Her father gave his head a tiny shake. "How do you know what Jonathan Schell says?"

"I read *The Fate of the Earth.*"

"Why? Where'd you get it?"

"From the shelves in your den. I had to do a nonfiction book report, so I picked that."

75

"That's no book for a fourteen-year-old to read. Did you even understand it?"

"Enough. He says that unless we change everything about how countries solve their differences, there will finally be a nuclear war. If four-year-olds bomb their own block cities, it must be the way people are. How can we change anything? How can we change it in time?"

"In time for what?"

"To keep us from destroying the earth."

"Whitney, are you exaggerating, or what? Are you really that afraid?"

Whitney only nodded.

Her father sighed and pushed himself off the floor with a slight grunt of effort. He stood looking down at her for a moment, shaking his head, and then sat on the bed beside her. For a moment they just sat there, almost but not quite touching; then he cleared his throat. "Whitney, I have to tell you first that I don't care what your reasons were, you had no right to do that to Jeremy. You scared him half to death and you might have done him serious damage. I don't think it would be right to let that go unpunished."

Whitney nodded again, squeezing the tissue in her hand.

"As for nuclear war—I don't know what to say to you, Whitney. Of course there's always the possibility of a nuclear war; as long as we have the capability, it could happen. But I don't think that a four-year-old's very natural violent play can be taken as a serious comment on the human race, any more than puppies roughhousing tell us that the adult dogs will be dangerous. You've lived your whole life in a nuclear world, Whit. So have I. And here I am; here you are. It hasn't happened yet. I can't believe that we or the Russians or any other nuclear power would be so utterly stupid as to purposely start a war no one could win—a war no one could even survive."

"Doesn't that worry you?"

Her father ran his hand through his hair. "Maybe it does, in an abstract way. But no more than dying. Some day I'll die. It's inevitable. I can't spend every waking minute thinking about it."

"This is more than one person dying. This is the end of the human race. There's a *difference*."

She watched her father closely. His face was creased and he rubbed at his chin. "Whitney, I'm a biologist. I know what the predictions are. Jonathan Schell didn't even know about 'nuclear winter' when he wrote that book, so he wasn't even aware of how likely extinction really is."

Whitney was crying again. "Then I don't see how you can just sit there so calmly."

"What good would it do for me to be something other than calm? Do you want me to run around like Chicken Little screaming that the end is coming? Death is inevitable, Whitney. Nuclear war is not."

"Just almost."

Her father put his arm around her. She should have felt comforted, but she didn't. "Do you have any idea how many major catastrophes there have been on this planet? Some scientists believe that we're on a cycle, colliding with comets or asteroids or giant meteors every twenty-six million years or so, and every time that happens, most of what's alive on earth dies out. Do you think human beings have any more right to continue than dinosaurs did? Do you think that just because we've been around a couple of million years—hardly any time at all in our planet's time scheme—we should go on forever? Where's your science, girl? There is no such thing as 'forever.'"

"Then what's the point?"

Her father shook his head. "I can't answer that. It's a question man's been asking and trying to answer probably ever since he realized he was alive, and would die. I have to believe in *life*, Whitney. Not human life—just life."

"You and Paul."

"And many others, Whitney. Life's incredibly tough. It can get set back to its earliest moments and begin all over again. Almost every living thing in a given age can be killed and new forms will appear and take over spaces that weren't available before. Do you think, if the dinosaurs hadn't been killed off, human beings would have evolved in the first place? We probably owe all these thousands of years of human civilization—for what they're worth—to a comet or whatever destroyed the dinosaurs. If human beings bring on the next catastrophe a few million years earlier than normal, what's the difference?"

"What's the difference? When it could happen during your lifetime? When it could happen tomorrow? Next year? Five years from now? While Jeremy's still a little kid? Before any of your children even have a chance to grow up?"

William Whitehurst stood up and spoke without looking at her. His voice was hard. Was he angry again? "There's no point in continuing this conversation, Whitney. I don't want a nuclear war. I'm not a madman. But I will not, I'm sure, be happy to die, either. And I'm not happy to know that you and Jeremy and Kate will die someday. That, too, could happen tomorrow or next year or five years from now. The only thing that's certain is uncertainty, Schell or no Schell." He turned back to her. "If you can't live with the prospect of death, you can't live." He went to the door and then stopped. "And you may not take out your fear on your brother. He has a right to throw balls at block cities. He's a little, little boy. And Whitney, you are not to mention nuclear war to him, do you understand?"

Whitney nodded.

"As for your punishment, you're grounded for two weeks."

And he was gone. Whitney, dry-eyed now, stared at the door that he had closed behind him. Was extinction the future of the human race, even without nuclear war? Was there really no question, then, except the question of individual death? Didn't it matter when anybody died? Or how many other people died at the same time? She shivered. Where was her science? he had asked. Nowhere, obviously. Nobody had ever told her about any catastrophe cycle. She didn't know about comets or what had killed the dinosaurs. All she knew was that she didn't want her world to end in the fireball of a nuclear explosion. She didn't want her world to end.

She wanted to apologize to Jeremy, but she couldn't make herself get up to find him. She could apologize later. Tomorrow. Jeremy was a good kid. He'd forgive her in a minute. She picked her pillow up from the floor and put it behind her, then slid down until she was on her back, staring up at the familiar ceiling. Whitney wished again that she were dead.

79

It was too late not to have been born. If you couldn't live without accepting death, then she couldn't live. Didn't want to. If she were dead, then the end wouldn't be ahead of her anymore—it couldn't surprise her. And if she were dead, it wouldn't matter how anyone else died. Or how many died. Or what was left. She wished, staring at her ceiling, that she were dead.

8

"What do you mean, grounded?" Paul asked. "Don't you remember what today is? The sci-fi convention. You promised to go with me. Whitney, how could you do this to me?"

Whitney, sitting on the floor in the upstairs hall, held the phone receiver away from her ear for a moment. "I'm sorry, Paul, I didn't do it on purpose."

"Do what? What could get you grounded for two whole weeks? Did you rob a bank?"

"I don't want to talk about it right now, okay?"

"But Whitney, it took me so long to convince you to go with me. I can't believe I'll have to go by myself now. I wanted you to go as Sarah Jane Smith."

"Who?"

"No, that's me."

"What?"

"Never mind. It was just a Whovian joke, Whit. You said, 'Who?' and I said, 'that's me.' I'm going as Dr. Who, see? I wanted you to be Sarah Jane—one of his sidekicks."

"Ask Allie to go with you."

"And pass up a Saturday afternoon with James Brady, wonderboy, are you kidding? I talked to her last night and he was her sole topic of conversation. Boring! They're doing

81

the library trip again this afternoon. Anyway, she's not into sci-fi."

"Neither am I, Paul. I mean, I only agreed to go to the convention with you because you were so pushy. I've only seen 'Dr. Who' about four times."

Paul's voice got lighter. "Never mind. I'll get you yet. What does grounding do to phone calls?"

"Limits them to ten minutes."

"Oh, terrific. I won't even be able to call you up tonight and tell you about it. No convention worth the name could be squeezed into ten minutes. That wouldn't even give me time to tell you about the costumes."

"There's always lunch hour at school next week." Whitney picked at the rug. She'd forgotten about the convention, but now she realized she'd actually been looking forward to it. "You can tell me during lunch hours."

Paul sighed. "Okay. No point in dwelling on how miserable I'll be having to go alone again. *Miserable*, Whit. But don't let that get you down. I'll survive it, somehow. I wish in the future you'd think about your obligations to your friends before you go and get yourself grounded. And you can tell your father I think he's medieval."

"Sure."

"Okay, now, Whit, since you aren't coming, I want to read you something. I was going to bring along *Hitchhiker's Guide* to lend to you, because you *have* to read it. The book gets its title from this electronic book that's like a travel guide to space. Across the front are the two most important words in the universe, 'DON'T PANIC.' You're panicking, Whitney. The earth is just one teeny little planet in space. There

82

are billions and trillions of others. And billions and trillions of life forms, most of them probably a lot more advanced than humans."

Whitney shook her head. "You believe that, don't you?"

"Well, why not? I can think of lots of dumber things to believe. I mean, Whit, there are people who believe that cows are their great-grandparents. I look up at the sky at night and I can't help but believe there're other people—or whatever—out there somewhere looking, too. You've gotta get over this thing you have that we're all there is."

"Even if we're not, I don't want us to quit." Kate went past on her way to the bathroom and pointed first at her watch and then down the stairs. Whitney nodded. "Listen, Paul, I've got to go. Time's nearly up."

"Oh, I forgot. Don't hang up yet. Did you see the morning paper? There's an article about the Old Place. Or rather, the estate. A woman sculptor bought it and is turning it into an art gallery. My mom says this woman's a big name, and that Martinsville is very lucky she came here. I'll bet she's the reason for that peacock."

"Thanks—I'll check the article out. I've got to hang up now, Paul. Have fun at the convention."

"Okay. Maybe I'll bring you a souvenir. Wish you could come, Whit—it'll be a gas, and that's exactly what you need right now. Don't forget to tell your dad he's medieval. See you Monday. Remember—DON'T PANIC!"

"Yeah." Whitney sat for a moment after hanging up. Kate had a flute lesson later and her mother had taken Jeremy to his tumbling class at the Y. Her father was playing tennis. She was the only one in the family with nothing to do, and she wasn't allowed to do anything anyway. One Whitney Whitehurst with nothing to do and no one to do it with. Grounded for two weeks, and practically suicidal. "Don't panic." Ha!

When she went into the kitchen, her father was there, dressed in his tennis clothes and reading the paper. She poured herself a bowl of cereal and got out the milk. She wished she had the nerve to tell him he was medieval. Maybe she deserved punishment for what she'd done to Jeremy, but it didn't have to be grounding. He didn't have to forbid her to do things with her friends. What kind of punishment was that, anyway? It punished Paul as much as it did her, and Paul hadn't done anything. He'd begged her for weeks to go to that convention with him, and now she was going to have to spend Saturday at home doing nothing and he was going to have to go by himself. She'd told her father exactly why she was feeling so bad, and he hadn't even tried to understand. If he'd understood, he'd never have grounded her.

Paul was right. She did need a sci-fi convention to get her mind off panicking. Now she was going to have another day all by herself in the house with nothing to do but brood. It would serve her father right if her mind cracked under the strain and she did something foolish. She might take a whole bottle of aspirin or something. Then he'd be sorry. Right now she needed her friends more than she'd ever needed them in her life, and right now her father had to decide to ground her. Why couldn't he have stopped her allowance? Money, she didn't need. Friends, she needed. She slammed her bowl down on the table.

Her father flipped his paper down and looked at her. "You trying to break the bowl or the table?"

"Very funny."

"Not exactly the tone of voice I'd associate with a repentant sinner."

"I'm serving my sentence. You didn't say I had to repent, too." Whitney poured the milk over her cereal and watched the flakes float to the top of the bowl. She avoided looking at him.

"Have you thought about what I told you last night? Are you still upset about nuclear war?"

What did he think? That the whole thing was so unimportant it could be wiped out in five minutes by a small lecture on the inevitability of extinction? "I guess not." She wasn't in the mood to hear another lecture. Better to let him think she was over it. Anyway, he was perfectly satisfied to think about a planet with nothing left but bacteria. How could he understand that for her it just wasn't enough?

"I knew I could rely on your good sense, once you thought about it."

She took a bite of cereal to avoid having to answer. He was so sure of his point of view, of the rightness of the way he thought about things, that he assumed she'd have to agree with him. That was probably the way he was with his students —just tell them "the truth" as he saw it, and that was that. Anybody with any brain would just have to accept it. Maybe all college professors were that way.

He flipped his paper up again and picked up his coffee cup. "You have any plans for today?"

"I *did*," she said, pointedly. "I was supposed to go to the science fiction convention at the student union with Paul. Now, of course, I can't go. He was very disappointed."

Her father snorted. "That boy is one strange kid. With a mind as good as his, he shouldn't be wasting his time with science fiction."

"He doesn't think of it as a waste."

"No, I suppose he doesn't. I think it's a copout. He doesn't have any friends, does he?"

"He has me—and Allie."

"That's what I mean. Two girls. That isn't quite normal for a fourteen-year-old boy."

"Paul isn't normal."

"That's what I said." Her father folded up the paper and looked at his watch. "Got to go. When your mother gets home, tell her I've got to go to the office this afternoon. I need to sort through some slides for my lecture Monday. I probably won't be back until supper."

When he'd left, Whitney picked up the paper and looked for the article Paul had told her about. On the first page of the local news section there was a photograph of Theodora Bourke standing in front of the estate. "Renowned Sculptor to Open Gallery," the headline said.

By the time she'd finished the article, Whitney knew what she would do with her morning. Maybe she couldn't go out with Paul or do anything with Allie, but nobody'd ever defined being grounded as being unable to visit Theodora Bourke. She left a note for her mother, yelled upstairs to tell Kate she was leaving, put two granola bars in her pocket, and set out for the Old Place.

86

Whitney sat on the stone in the gazebo, eating a granola bar. Theodora Bourke wasn't there, and neither, as far as she could tell, was the peacock. The only sounds of activity came from the big house. She wanted to go up there, but she didn't quite have the nerve. It was one thing to come here, hoping to run into the woman, but something else entirely actually to go looking for her. Theodora Bourke didn't give the impression of being fond of casual visitors.

Anyway, it was pretty here, and much better than being at home alone. The sun filtered down through the new leaves and tinted everything a yellowish green. Birds sang and squirrels scurried through the litter of dead leaves on the ground. A black swallowtail butterfly flitted in through the doorway of the gazebo, danced briefly around Whitney's head while she sat, holding her breath. The sun caught the iridescence of its purple wings. If a butterfly landed on you, it meant good luck, and she could use a little luck. After a moment, though, it zigged and zagged and disappeared through a large hole in the latticework. Whitney supposed it had been too much to hope for. She could hardly be mistaken for a flower, which had to be what the butterfly was looking for.

She took a deep breath, and breathed in the smell of spring. What was it exactly? There was damp earth in it, and old leaves, but also something sweet and very green, as if the distinction had gotten blurred between sight and smell. The smell of green. It had to be one of the best smells in the world. All of a sudden, she knew she didn't really wish to be dead. Not now, at least. Last night it had seemed so much better than being afraid. But today, surrounded by sunlight and butterflies, death was all wrong, like closing a door against everything beautiful. If she were dead she couldn't experience the smell or the light—she couldn't watch that butterfly's strange, jagged flight.

Allie was always calling her a pessimist, always telling her that when a glass was half full, she insisted on calling it half empty. Well, not today. There was nothing half empty about this moment, even if she was alone with it. Not even if the world that provided such moments wouldn't last another five years. She pushed that thought away. Not here. Not today.

She shivered. The rock was cold under her and the roof of the gazebo, in spite of its holes, created too much shade. She went out into the sunlight and stood, leaning against a tree, listening. If she pretended not to hear the occasional truck going past the estate, and the hammering from the house, she could imagine herself in a forest. "The forest primeval." She wondered what it had been like here in this very spot before people came, when there had been only trees and vines and butterflies. No roses, of course—those had been planted. Wild ones, maybe. And what animals had been here before human beings? Deer? Bear? Rabbits and squirrels? Saber-toothed tigers? Woolly mammoths? Had there been woolly mammoths in Pennsylvania before people had come to this continent? She was suddenly aware that something—or someone—was crunching through the leaves. Goose bumps rose along her arms, and she turned to see Theodora Bourke, dressed exactly as she had been before.

"Do you know which bird it is that keeps shouting 'perty,

perty, perty'?" Theodora Bourke asked, apparently not at all surprised to find her there.

Whitney listened. It *did* sound a little like that. "I think it's a cardinal." She looked into the trees, trying to find the direction the birdcall was coming from. Somewhere off to the left the call was answered. Then it changed to a different set of notes, also answered, and finally it went back to "perty, perty, perty" again. It was then that she saw it, and pointed. The red of the cardinal stood out brilliantly against the pale green tassels of the tree flowers behind it.

"I see it," the woman said. "Beautiful birds."

Whitney nodded.

"Less spectacular than peacocks. But I like them." She took off her leather work gloves, tucked them under one arm, and rubbed her hands together. Whitney thought she'd never seen a woman with such powerful-looking hands. "The gloves are supposed to provide protection, but I think I'm getting blisters anyway. And blisters on the blisters."

"I saw the article about you in the paper this morning," Whitney said.

"Ah, yes. 'Renowned Sculptor,' they called me. So—did you come for an autograph?"

Whitney couldn't tell if she was serious or teasing her. She felt suddenly very shy. "No—not exactly . . ." What had she come for, anyway? To see some of the sculptures, to see what a famous person was like, maybe. Could she say that? Hardly. "I was interested in your work. In what you do, and—oh— what you're going to do with this place."

"Gallery in the big house with my apartment upstairs.

Studio in the carriage house. Garden. That's it. I thought maybe you'd come to get a taste of spring."

Whitney grinned. "That, too. Except I didn't know I'd come for that until I got here. It's so beautiful, I was thinking that right here the glass is full."

"What?"

Whitney felt her cheeks getting hot. What a dumb thing to say! "You know that saying about the optimist and pessimist? About whether the glass is half full or half empty?"

"And you think it's full? Completely full? What does that make you?"

"Crazy, I guess. Anyway, I'm usually one of the people who thinks it's half empty. It's just right here and now that it seems full."

The woman looked around her, up toward the tops of the trees, then down to the vines twining upward. "Too full, actually. I've spent days tearing out vines and poison ivy—even roses. Everything's growing—too much and too fast. I'd settle for half right now—even half empty." Then she glanced at the gazebo. "It's a good thing you're not being a pessimist today. I suspect that even negative psychic vibrations could knock that down. I'd rather like to keep it yet awhile. I'm getting to like it."

"I'll try not to think bad things at it."

"Good. Now, I've got to get back to work. If I stop for ten minutes there are hundreds of new vines to tear out by the time I get back." She put her gloves back on and then looked at Whitney as if appraising her. "How strong are you?"

"I don't know. But I'm pretty good at arm wrestling."

"How would you like to help me get rid of the largest yew bush—tree—in the world?"

"Okay," Whitney answered, without even thinking about it.

The woman turned and stalked off without another word. Whitney stood for a moment, and then followed her. They stepped over creepers and skirted masses of rosebush and came out of the woods near the old carriage house. Two pickup trucks were parked in the circular driveway, one filled with lumber and sheetrock, the other containing an enormous, built-in tool box. A table was set up, with an orange extension cord snaking off and disappearing through an open window of the mansion. The sound of hammering was coming from inside, and an occasional male voice could be heard. Theodora Bourke disappeared through a door in the side of the carriage house, and Whitney followed. The inside of the building was like a barn, two full stories high near the gigantic double doors. In the back half a loft split the space, creating a lower and an upper level. Standing against the walls in the massive open space were seven huge shapes, covered with pieces of canvas. In the darker section under the loft were stacks of boxes and crates and some machines, also covered, their lower parts showing under the cloths. This was going to be the studio. Whitney wondered what it would be like when it was finished, when Theodora was doing her work. The newspaper had said that there were "Bourke pieces" in several New York museums and in many shopping malls and city parks. Were the shapes under the cloths her sculptures? She wanted to see them, but she didn't have the nerve to ask.

91

"These will be too big, but they'll have to do. You can't work with your bare hands." Theodora Bourke came out of a small, shedlike room under the edge of the loft and handed her a pair of leather gloves. Then she went back and came out with a new-looking pair of long-handled pruning shears, a bow saw, and an axe. "We'll probably have to use all of these."

With that, she went back outside. Whitney, wishing she had the nerve to peek under one of the cloths, reluctantly went out after her.

"There's your friend, Raj."

Whitney looked where the woman was pointing and saw the peacock coming around one of the trucks. His tail dragged behind him in the dirt and sawdust, and she wanted to tell him to pick it up. "He needs someone to carry his train for him," she said.

"He picks it up himself if there's mud. Otherwise, he just lets it follow him. Maybe he'll display for us. There's nothing in the world quite like it."

They watched for a while, but the peacock paid no attention to them at all. It merely walked along, dragging its tail, occasionally pecking the ground in front of it as if it expected to find something edible there.

"No point in standing around waiting. He'll display when he feels like it and not before. Let's get to work." She led the way to a vast yew bush that had completely blocked what was left of a stone pathway leading into the woods. It really was more of a tree than a bush. She handed the pruning shears to Whitney. "You take these and start lopping off branches. You can probably manage anything less than—

92

oh—an inch and a half across, I guess. I'll go to work on the trunks." She paused. "It's Whitney, isn't it?"

"Yes." Whitney was flattered that she'd remembered her name.

"Right. Keep in mind, Whitney, that we aren't pruning now. We're chopping. We're getting rid of it entirely, so just start anywhere. This is the only way to deal with anything that's gotten so badly overgrown. I'll put something else in its place later—something that's guaranteed not to grow more than two feet."

For the next two hours they cut and sawed and chopped. When Theodora Bourke sawed through a large branch, Whitney clipped all the smaller branches off and laid them in a pile, tips facing the same direction. The pile grew so tall, finally, that she had to start another or it would have toppled over. Whitney, too, began to think her blisters were growing blisters. Where she had to press the hardest on the handles of the pruning shears, her palms ached and burned. Her back ached from stretching and bending, and her wrists were scratched, leaving little dotted trails of blood between the tops of the gloves and where her jacket sleeves had gotten pushed up. They talked little, concentrating on the work at hand. Whitney was just as glad about the talking, because she didn't think she'd be able to think of anything to say. She was acutely conscious that the woman who worked beside her was famous. It was a very strange feeling.

The sun was warm on her body, though, and there was a toughness to the job that eventually made her forget everything except the job itself. She learned quickly how to angle the shears so they'd cut directly through a branch instead of

93

crushing and tearing at it, and she also learned quickly how thick a branch she could manage. A few times she'd had to rest one long handle on the ground and push down on the other with both hands and all her weight to cut all the way through. After that, she didn't bother to try the bigger branches. Theodora would get those with the saw if they needed to be cut. Branch after branch came down and got trimmed and then stacked.

Once a man came out of the house to ask some questions. It was funny to see the woman, in her work clothes and heavy gloves, a saw dangling from one hand, looking down into the face of the shorter man. He was broad-shouldered and strong-looking, or would have looked strong anywhere else. Next to the Amazon, Whitney thought, he looked squat and awkward.

There was still one major trunk left, its dark, needle-covered branches all leaning out across the path, its exposed side bare and vulnerable in the sun, when Theodora groaned, laid the saw on the ground and stretched. She reached upward toward the sky, then folded in the middle and touched her toes. "Break time," she said. "Would you like some lunch?"

Whitney glanced at her watch and saw that it was after one. Her second granola bar was still in her jeans pocket, and she hadn't even thought of food. "Yes, please," she said, and put down the pruning sheers. She flexed her hands and pulled off her gloves. Both palms were red. Now that she'd let go of the shears, both hands hurt. So did her arms. The scratches tingled.

"We can wash up a little at the hose. The cold water will feel good. The water's not on in the house."

They went to the side of the carriage house where a hose was coiled around a hook, and washed their hands. Theodora leaned over and took a drink, then let the water play all over her face, wetting her hair. When she stood up, the water dripped onto her shirt, but she seemed not to notice. "Want a drink? A face wash?"

"Just a drink, thanks." Whitney took the hose and carefully got a drink. "I can go home for lunch," she said, suddenly shy again. If there was no water on in the house, how could they have lunch there?

"After all you've done, the least I can provide is some sustenance. Will it be all right with your folks, do you think?"

"I guess so. We're pretty casual about lunch on Saturday. Everybody fends for himself—except my baby brother."

"Is a sandwich from the deli okay? Pastrami on rye?"

"Sure."

"Let's go, then."

Again, Whitney found herself following the expanse of plaid-covered back, this time around the side of the house to where a battered Volkswagon van was parked in the driveway. Theodora got into the driver's side and Whitney got in on the right. There were only the two front seats in the van. Behind them the space was littered with old blankets and boxes. In an open box behind the driver's seat were gardening books.

"My library," Theodora explained as she turned the ignition key. The engine growled, caught, died, and growled again. After several tries, it ran steadily, if not smoothly, and they moved down the driveway to the street. "I borrowed this van from a friend. Never had a car in the City, but that's going to have to change. Meantime, this is just what I need."

They went to the deli and ordered sandwiches. Whitney could hardly believe that a woman, particularly a "renowned sculptor," would go out in public with wet hair, a damp shirt, and mud all over her boots. Her mother wouldn't so much as walk across the street looking like that. People did notice Theodora Bourke. Whitney had the feeling they'd notice her anyway, though, even if she were dressed in a conservative suit. She just seemed to command attention. It's not only her size, either, Whitney thought, because the noticing had a kind of respectful interest to it. Theodora Bourke, for her part, didn't seem to notice anyone except the round, mustached man behind the counter, from whom she ordered their food. She got two hot pastrami on ryes and two imported ginger ales.

"Do you mind if we take them back and eat them at the house?"

Whiney shook her head. "It's probably better that way. My dad comes here for lunch sometimes, and I'm supposed to be grounded. I don't know what would happen if he saw me here."

"Grounded?" Theodora Bourke smiled. "I wondered why you took on such a tough job so easily. An alternative to Saturday at home alone?"

Whitney shrugged. "Sort of. I've liked doing it, though. Really."

They took their food back then, and didn't talk further until they were both seated on upturned crates at a workbench in the carriage house. Theodora had spread newspaper out as a tablecloth. "Is your sandwich okay?" she asked.

Whitney nodded. It was more than okay. It might be the

best sandwich she had tasted in her life. She even liked the ginger ale. Usually, she hated imported ginger ale—it always tasted bitter. Not today, though. It was just right with the sandwich.

As Whitney ate, she looked at the shrouded machines, and the other shapes that might be sculptures. Not once had Theodora Bourke mentioned her work, except to acknowledge the newspaper article. Whitney wondered why. She really wanted to see it, but still couldn't get up the nerve to ask. Maybe after lunch, she thought, the woman would offer to show her what was under the cloths. She'd wait, anyway, until the offer was made. It was all very strange, really, the way they'd worked without talking, the way they were eating now without talking. Theodora Bourke seemed to want Whitney's help, and was glad of her company, too, maybe. But there was a kind of a fence around her, warning trespassers to keep out. She'd share her garden, but maybe not herself.

"Thank you very much," Whitney said when she'd finished her sandwich.

Theodora had been staring off toward the open door of the carriage house as she ate. Now she looked at Whitney, and her dark eyes were as impenetrable as a wall. "The least I could do is feed you. You've been working like a Trojan."

"It's been fun—sort of."

The woman smiled and flexed her hands. "Except for the pain?"

Whitney looked at her hands and then grinned. "Yeah. And what's a little pain after all?"

"Right. What's a little pain?" She looked away again and

97

grew very still. After a moment, with a slight shake of her shoulders, Theodora Bourke stood up and began rolling the newspapers. Napkins and sandwich wrappers disappeared as she rolled, and Whitney picked up the empty soda cans. They dropped the trash into a can next to the workbench. "That's the way I like to clean up after lunch!" Theodora stretched again, touched her toes again, rubbed at her lower back, and groaned. "Are you done for or shall we tackle the last of that infernal monster? You said you were grounded. Will you get in trouble for being here?"

Whitney shrugged. "I don't really know. Nothing like this has come up before. When I'm grounded I can't go out with my friends or have long phone calls. Nobody's ever said a thing about chopping up bushes."

"I imagine not. You want to call home?"

"I don't think so. I left my mother a note, so she knows where I am. I'd rather just leave it the way it is. Anyway, Dad's not going to be home till later."

"And the grounding was his idea?"

Whitney nodded. "He'd probably think it's good for me to be working instead of watching television or something."

"All right, then, let's get at it."

For three more hours they worked, and when they were done the pile of branches was at least twelve feet long and nearly four feet high. Where the yew had stood was a huge ring of bare ground, in the middle of which were the sawed-off stumps of the many-branched trunk.

They stood together, surveying their work. "Who'd have thought that bush would make such a pile?"

"It didn't look that big," Whitney said.

"I'll have to hire someone to pull out the stump, I suppose. The roots probably reach halfway to China."

Whitney took off her gloves and handed them to Theodora. "Thanks for these. I couldn't have done it without them."

"I'm the one who should be doing the thanking. This job would have taken me the whole weekend alone." She looked around. "Now I can do some planting tomorrow—a few azaleas and some summer bulbs. I'm nowhere nearly finished with the cutting back and clearing out, but I'm tired of destroying things. I want to put in new life instead of just tearing out the old."

"You must know a lot about gardening."

Theodora Bourke laughed a deep, throaty laugh. "I know about as much as a New Yorker can be expected to know. Which is approximately zilch. Philodendrons I know. And fig trees and rubber plants and Boston ferns. Anything that looks elegant in an apartment or a show window. This outdoor stuff is all new to me. But I've got my library."

"Couldn't you just hire a gardener?"

"I could. But then I wouldn't be doing it. This is something I want to do myself."

Before Whitney could ask why, the peacock came out of the woods, directly toward them, walking slowly along the newly uncovered stone path. He saw them and stopped. For a moment Whitney thought he was going to turn around and go back, but he only tipped his head slightly. His feet, she thought, were remarkably big and ugly. They didn't seem to go with the feathers of his neck and head that caught the sunlight and glowed blue and then green as he moved. Suddenly, he began to shake himself all over, and his tail

99

began to rise behind him, the feathers fanning out until they formed a quivering half-circle, like a gigantic halo behind his head. Before Whitney had had a chance to really see his display, he turned his back on them, still vibrating his tail, and left them looking at the drab backs of his tail feathers and a little puff of shorter feathers that looked like grubby underwear. Whitney started after him, wanting to get around to the other side to see the display from the front, but Theodora put her hand on her arm and stopped her. "Wait."

Whitney waited. After quivering his tail at the empty woods for a while, the peacock turned back toward them, stepping slowly and carefully, with great dignity. As he turned, the sun caught the coppers and golds and iridescent blues and greens of his plumes, and Whitney caught her breath. She had never seen anything so beautiful in her whole life. While the bird continued his display, she didn't breathe. It was almost, she thought, like watching a burst of fireworks that kept on, that didn't fade and disappear, so that the "oohs" and "aahs" of the watching crowd had to go on and on. It was incredibly, astonishingly, impossibly gorgeous.

And then, as suddenly as it had begun, it was over. The bird simply folded the feathers up again, let them down, and walked off, dragging the glory behind him in the dirt. Whitney drew in a deep, deep breath. She felt as if she'd just come up from swimming too far underwater.

"That's why I bought him. People have told me terrible things about peacocks. But how could I resist that?"

"Where did you get him?" Whitney asked.

"From a man whose wife was tired of him. Peacocks eat

flowers and scream. I think the woman must have been blind."

"He's wonderful," Whitney said, thinking that the word didn't say enough. She couldn't imagine a word for what she'd just seen.

"Yes."

A breeze blew across the back of Whitney's neck. The sun was lower in the sky than she'd realized. She glanced at her watch and saw that it was nearly five o'clock. "I'd better go now," she said reluctantly. "Thank you for today."

"And thank you, Whitney. If I didn't think you'd already done too much, I'd suggest you drop by tomorrow. At least then I'll be doing something that will be pretty when I'm done."

Whitney didn't even pause to think about it. "I'd love to help plant," she said. "If Dad'll let me come."

Theodora Bourke smiled, and for a moment Whitney thought the fences seemed to be down. "Then I'll see you tomorrow. If you don't come, I'll know your father put his foot down."

"Okay. Good-bye."

Whitney hurried home, hoping no one would mind that she'd been gone so long, hoping they'd let her come back tomorrow. When she got inside the front door, she knew everything was all right. The house was empty. A note on the refrigerator said that her mother had taken Jeremy and Kate shopping for summer clothes. Whitney grinned. Her father hadn't been home yet.

As she started up the stairs, Whitney became overpoweringly aware of how tired she was. Every muscle in her body ached, and she could hardly lift her feet. She grabbed the banister to pull herself up and groaned. The blisters on her hands made it feel almost as if the banister were made of hot metal. When she got to her room, she sat down on the bed, and even sitting hurt. She leaned to look into the small open space of her mirror. Her face was streaked with dirt, her hair was tangled with bits of yew twig. She looked as if she'd been rolling in dirt. Slowly, pushing herself carefully to her feet, she got up and headed for the bathroom. She needed to have a shower before anyone got home. She hoped a hot shower would take away some of the pain and wake her up a little. For the first time in her life, she was tired enough to go to bed without bothering to eat supper.

❦ 9 ❦

Whitney stood under the shower and let the hot water pour down on her head. The force of the water and the heat felt good, but she was so tired she could hardly stay on her feet. Quickly, she soaped her body and rinsed; then she sat down in the tub and wrapped her arms around her knees. The water pummeled her head and back, much harder now that it fell from so far above. She tilted her head back just enough to let the water run over her face, catching some in her mouth and letting it run out again. If it weren't for the warmth, she could imagine herself under a waterfall. She squeezed her eyes tightly shut and tried to see it—a waterfall on a tropical island. She was sitting at the edge of a deep, clear pool lined with black volcanic rock. Around the pool grew ferns and philodendrons and palms. Brilliantly colored tropical birds called from the trees above, occasionally flying past, the sun catching their green and scarlet feathers. Around her was a jungle, its green depths lit in patches by the filtered sun, orchids growing among its shadows. The air was warm and damp and the sun hot, as hot as the shower water that pounded against her now.

It had been a very strange day, Whitney thought. In the

cool Pennsylvania spring she had felt the same kind of warmth and life she could visualize on her imaginary tropical island. She'd been surrounded by life—the cardinals, the squirrels, sparrows, and butterflies, the yew tree itself, and, of course, Raj. Theodora Bourke, too. Her energy was catching. The whole day had been spent killing something, really—chopping down that incredible bush that had turned into a tree. But it hadn't felt that way. She'd gone from wishing she were dead to feeling more alive, maybe, than she'd ever felt before. She moved a little to direct the water at her lower back. Maybe she'd felt more alive because she'd become aware of muscles she'd never noticed before. She turned her hands over and looked at her reddened palms; small white circles had appeared at the bases of her fingers. Blisters on her blisters, Theodora Bourke had said. Why did it make her feel good to look at them? Maybe because they were proof of the day, proof that what she'd done hadn't been as imaginary as her jungle waterfall. They'd actually accomplished something together, she and the "renowned sculptor," who'd treated her as an equal. She remembered the feeling she'd had when they were finished, looking at the stump, at the huge pile of cut branches. Imagine feeling that proud of having cut down a bush. Crazy.

And Raj. She didn't care whether peacocks were nice or not, whether they screamed or ate flowers or what they did. They had such astonishing tails. Whitney hugged her knees more tightly and rested her chin on them, so the water was pounding on her shoulders just where they felt the stiffest. She took a deep breath of the warm, steamy air and let it out slowly, feeling her whole body relax into the heat. Theodora Bourke had quoted somebody who'd called a peacock's tail a map of the universe. Whitney had always thought of those circles as eyes, before. But couldn't they be suns? And planets? Glowing and changing color the way they did, they seemed to generate light on their own.

Why, Whitney wondered, was the peacock's tail so beautiful? Her father talked about evolution a lot, about how a change in one species of plant or animal connected with another—flowers developing the scent of a female wasp to lure a male wasp to come track through their pollen and spread it around, a spider whose color and shape exactly imitated a heather blossom so it could lie in wait for the insects that came to the heather for the nectar. But that was all so practical. It didn't explain beauty. Why were flowers beautiful? Why were butterflies? Why was a spider's web, spangled with dewdrops, so lovely that jewelers copied it with gold and diamonds? In all her father's admiring talk about how life adapted itself, she couldn't ever remember him trying to account for beauty.

If Raj's tail was meant to attract a mate, why did it attract Theodora and Whitney and all the people who collected the tail feathers and used them to decorate their houses? And even if a flower's colors and scents were just runway markers to guide a bee to its pollen, why did human beings respond to flowers the way they did? Why did people plant gardens and interfere with evolution by breeding roses? Everything in nature wasn't beautiful—there were stink bugs and skunk cabbage and some oozy, disgusting kinds of fungus. Why did people distinguish between ugly and beautiful? And why did they choose beauty?

Something didn't fit. Could all the eons of life and evolution that led to flowers and butterflies and the tails of peacocks have been created just to be snuffed out in a nuclear war? Did God mean everything, all the astonishing complexity of life, as a cruel joke? The water pounding down on her was not as hot as before. Whitney tipped her head back again and got another mouthful of water—barely warm on her tongue. She swallowed it and sighed. She didn't want to get out of the tub. But she didn't want to sit there with cold water pouring down on her, either. She stood up, the rapidly cooling water cascading over her, and stretched. It wasn't God's fault if the same human beings who could make gardens and music and sculpture also made bombs and missiles. It was people who made everything a cruel joke, people who were willing to destroy a world that had in it a bird with a map of the universe on its tail. She turned off the water, stepped out of the tub, and began to towel herself dry.

"You are never going to guess what happened this afternoon." Allie's voice sounded breathless over the phone. "Never in a million years."

Whitney rubbed at her hair with a towel and tried to decide what could make Allie's voice sound that way. It could hardly take a million years to guess. "James Brady either kissed you or asked you to the spring ball. Or both."

"Whitney Whitehurst, I hate you!"

"I thought we were best friends."

"That doesn't keep me from hating you. You guessed it. Both. First he kissed me . . ."

"French kiss?"

"Whitney! No. Just a—just a regular kiss."

"One among millions. Did he catch his lip in your braces?"

"Will you stop? Will you take this seriously for just one minute, please?"

Whitney giggled. "Okay. Seriously. And then he asked you to the spring ball."

"Yes."

"There. Your story's all told. That wasn't so hard, was it? And now there can be a nuclear war because you'll have had your one heavy date."

Allie screeched and Whitney had to hold the phone away. "What is with you today, Whit?"

"I'm grounded, I couldn't go with Paul to that sci-fi convention, and the world's going to end." For some reason, Whitney didn't mention Theodora Bourke. She wanted to keep this day to herself for a while.

"Grounded? How long?"

"Two weeks."

"I'll die!" Allie said. "I wanted you to come with me to pick out my dress."

"I can do that when my sentence is up."

"But the ball's in a month. There won't be time."

Whitney shook her head. "Do you mean to say you can't find a dress in two weeks?"

"It's me, remember? The jolly thin giant. What if I can't find anything that fits? There has to be time to have it altered."

"There'll be time. You'd think you were planning an assault on Everest instead of going to a dance. We'll shop when the prison term's up. If the world lasts that long."

107

"Oh, I forgot. James says you're having an existential depression."

"A what?"

"Existential depression. He says I should watch you very carefully because when people have existential depressions, they commit suicide sometimes. You haven't been thinking about suicide, have you, Whit?"

Whitney thought about last night. And again this morning. About the bottle of aspirins. "No. Are you kidding? Do you think I'm crazy?"

Allie giggled. "You want the truth?"

"Never mind. Listen, our time's up, and I've got to go, anyway. It's dinnertime. Tell your new boyfriend that I'm only partly crazy. I'm very fond of being alive."

"Okay. 'Bye."

"'Bye." As Whitney hung up the phone, she sighed. She was fond of being alive, all right. Wasn't that the problem in the first place? She wanted the world to go on. She wanted everybody to stay alive.

"Theodora Bourke?" Whitney's father put his fork down and looked quizzically at Whitney. "The sculptor who was written up in the paper? How'd you meet her?"

"You remember the Old Place? Where Paul and Allie and I used to play when we were little?"

"That broken-down gazebo?" her father asked.

"Yeah. We took you there one time to show you when we'd made it into a castle."

"Castle? Where's a castle?" Jeremy asked around a mouthful of meatloaf.

"It isn't a real one," Kate told him. "You had to have a terrific imagination even to pretend it was."

"Oh, pooh. I wanted there to be a castle."

"That's the estate that's being turned into a gallery?" Marianne Whitehurst asked. "I read that article, but didn't make the connection. I was too busy wondering why a major artist of any kind would want to set up a gallery in this town."

William Whitehurst set his wine glass down hard. "I can't see why this isn't as good a place for a gallery as any. Look at Woodstock, New York, for heaven's sake. Who'd have picked that for an art colony? It was just an ordinary town till some artists moved there. The same goes for any of them. Why Sausalito? Why Martha's Vineyard? Why anywhere?"

"You don't honestly think Martinsville is going to become an art colony," Kate said.

"I didn't say that. I only said that there's no reason it couldn't be. And no reason why a decently cultured college town can't support one good art gallery."

"All right, all right," Marianne Whitehurst said. "I certainly don't have anything against it. It just seemed unusual that a woman who had had a gallery in New York City would leave it all of a sudden and come here."

"I can't see how an artist could survive in New York City in the first place," Kate said. "All that pollution and noise and all those muggers. What's beautiful about New York? How can an artist do any decent work if there isn't anything beautiful?"

Whitney thought about her imaginary island again, and the green jungle full of orchids. New York certainly couldn't offer much in the way of gardens or peacocks.

109

"The museums," Marianne Whitehurst said. "There are all those museums. And galleries. It seems to me if you care about art there isn't a better place to be than New York. When was the last time you saw a masterpiece in Martinsville? You certainly don't find masterpieces at the sidewalk fair in the fall. Last year somebody won first place for a still life that looked as if it had been painted in a fun house mirror!"

"I don't mean beauty like in other art. I mean a beautiful environment," Kate said. "At least here the streets are pretty. All those old cobblestones we still have, and the trees making a roof over the streets. All those townhouses people have fixed up, and the little parks. Even estates like the one she's turning into a gallery. And the campus. That's beautiful. What's beautiful like that in New York? All concrete and glass. Ugh."

William Whitehurst turned back to Whitney. "You still haven't answered my original question. How'd you meet Theodora Bourke?"

"I went over to the Old Place with Paul last week. . . ."

"Oh yeah?" Kate said, grinning knowingly. "Still making castles? Or are you two finally growing up?"

Whitney felt the blood rise in her cheeks. Did sixteen-year-olds think of nothing except sex? "We just went to see if it was still there, just to see it."

"Right." Kate didn't change her expression. "An exercise in nostalgia."

"What's noss—nosstall—what Kate said?" Jeremy asked.

"Memory," his mother said. "Let her alone, Kate."

"And we saw a peacock. So I went back to see if I could

110

find the peacock, and Theodora Bourke was working on the garden."

"And she asked you to come work for her today?"

"No, Dad. She just said I could come back whenever I wanted. She said she'd had a place like that when she was my age and it meant a lot to her."

"What's she like?" Kate asked. "Is she snobby or nice? I never met anybody famous."

"She's . . . I don't know. I can't describe her—except that she's tall. She doesn't *act* famous. She's just—just herself."

"Does she wear really neat, artsy clothes? And lots of makeup and big dangly earrings? I mean, if I saw her on the street, would I know she was an artist?"

"She wears jeans. At least that's what she had on the first time I saw her and again today. But she's been working in the garden. You wouldn't expect her to wear makeup and earrings to do that."

"I wouldn't expect her to work in a garden at all," Kate said. "Why isn't she sculpting?"

"I don't know." Whitney thought of the carriage house, with its mysterious, draped forms. "She's turning the carriage house into her studio."

"So how'd you end up helping her today?" her father asked.

"Well, everybody was going off today, and I didn't have anything to do, so I went over there. I guess I was kind of hoping to see her again, once I'd read that article. Anyway, she was there, and she asked if I wanted to help her cut down this enormous yew tree that was blocking the path into the garden. She gave me a pair of leather gloves and we cut it down and chopped it up. It took the whole day. Except we

111

stopped for lunch. She got me a sandwich at the deli. She said it was the least she could do for the help I was giving her."

William Whitehurst frowned. "I'm surprised she didn't offer to pay you. She can't be exactly poor."

"I didn't want money, Dad. I just wanted to help. You should have seen how big that tree was." She held up her hands. "I got blisters in spite of the gloves. It was really hard work, but I liked it."

"I wish you'd like hard work around here, young lady. I get nothing but grief when I dare to suggest you mow the lawn."

Marianne Whitehurst shook her head. "It's always easier to do work for someone else than it is at home. I always used to wash dishes for people when I babysat, but my mother had to force me to do them at home."

"The truth is out!" Kate said. "You weren't perfect."

"Of course I was. Except for that small fault. And anyway" —Marianne Whitehurst glared at her older daughter—"I did them, which is more than we can say about some people around here sometimes."

"I do them!" Kate said. "Eventually."

"So what's the rest of the story?" William Whitehurst asked.

Whitney looked at her father. "What do you mean?"

"Are you planning to help her again?"

"She asked if I could come help her plant tomorrow. Mostly she's getting rid of all the junk that's grown over the garden. But she says she wants to get some planting done so she isn't just killing things all the time. Tomorrow she's

112

putting in some azaleas and stuff. I didn't promise to help because I didn't know if you'd let me."

"Well, you *are* grounded."

"I don't think this could be put in the same category as going out with Paul and Allie."

Whitney smiled at her mother. She'd been hoping her mother would see it her way.

"I suppose there is a difference," her father said. "At least she'd be working."

"And for Theodora Bourke."

"Mother," Kate said. "That's awful. You sound like a celebrity worshipper or something."

"Who wanted to know if she dressed like an artist? Couldn't be that you're the tiniest bit jealous?"

"Pure intellectual curiosity," Kate replied. "Anyway, how could I be jealous of chopping trees and scrabbling around in the dirt?"

"Well, all right," William Whitehurst said, at last. "You can help her if you want."

"But since I'm grounded, I should be very careful not to have any fun," Whitney said, grinning.

"Don't press your luck, kid. I haven't forgotten what you did to Jeremy."

"What'd she do? What'd she do to me?"

Whitney laughed. That was just like Jeremy. Shrieking his head off, acting as if he were dying, and the next day not even remembering what had happened.

"Never mind. You don't have to remember it. I do," their father said.

"Right." Kate made a ferocious face. "Observe the father

113

figure maintaining discipline, wearing the pants, molding our characters. Just like in olden times."

"That's enough out of you. You can clear the table."

"We haven't had our dessert yet!" Jeremy wailed.

"All right, then. Get the dessert."

Whitney looked around the table at her family. Sometimes they were terrific. How could anyone want to die when they had a family? Kate took a half gallon container of Oreo mint ice cream out of the refrigerator, and Whitney grinned to herself. How could anyone want to die when there was Oreo mint ice cream for dessert?

❦ 10 ❦

They had worked in silence most of the morning, nothing breaking it except the sound of the rented rototiller Theodora used to prepare the soil for the beds of azaleas they were planting, or a few words telling Whitney what to do. There was a comfort to the silence, though, as if they were sharing something that didn't need words, something that was about doing rather than talking. A strange communication, Whitney thought, as she pushed the soil around the woody stem of an azalea plant that was just beginning to show thin slices of red at the edges of its flower buds. They could hear other kinds of communication all around them, from the birds particularly. Whitney didn't know what they were saying to each other, those birds that would sit on a branch and repeat the same phrases over and over, listening in the intervals for those phrases to be repeated from somewhere else. There were echoes and repetitions everywhere. Mating and territories, she supposed. That's what it was all about. And she wondered again about beauty. The cardinals made such pretty sounds, but the starlings rasped their notes harshly, and the chickadees sounded as if they were quarreling incessantly. It was surprising that the combination of all those different voices was so pleasant.

She was beginning to see how the driveway would look, even though they'd made only the barest beginning. Theodora had tilled the soil in the center of the driveway and then all the way around the outer edges as well. They had removed the clumps of grass from the tilled soil, raked out lumps and rocks, hoed and raked peat moss into the soil and mixed in fertilizer before they'd begun to plant. The azaleas stood in their rusty metal containers around the driveway where they were to be planted and in a clump in the center. Bags of pine bark mulch were stacked next to the van, ready to spread when the planting was finished.

Now Theodora was digging the holes for the plants, gently dislodging them from their containers and setting them in place. Whitney was following, filling the holes and packing the dirt tightly around the roots. Some of the plants were beginning to bloom already, but some weren't showing even a hint of the color they would be. Each had a plastic tag, and Whitney tried to imagine the color of each plant's blossoms. "Holly red" was easy. And "snowflake." But what was the difference between "pink pearl" and something called "pink pericat"?

She finished tamping down the soil around her "holly red" plant and sat back on her heels with a sigh. She took off her leather gloves for a moment and looked at the palms of her hands. The blisters had gone down some, but her hands were still sore. The gloves made working awkward, but using her bare hands hurt too much. She'd heard somewhere about farmers who loved the feel of the soil in their hands, so she'd tried crumbling some of the lumps. It just hurt. Loving the feel of the soil had to be someone's romantic idea. She couldn't imagine a Kansas wheat farmer, used to doing everything with huge machines, messing around in the dirt with his bare hands.

She moved to the next plant, put her gloves back on, and began pushing the dirt and peat moss mixture into the hole. A worm wriggled in the dirt pile, bits of black peat moss stuck to its pinky-brown skin. She picked it up and put it into the hole, thinking it would dry out and die in the sun. It was lucky it hadn't been chopped by the rototiller. She wondered how many had been killed getting the garden ready for planting. Worms were supposed to be good for gardens, she knew—did the tilling kill enough to make a difference? And what did the fertilizer do to worms? Did it stick to their skins like the peat moss and then burn them? Theodora had explained that they needed to mix the fertilizer well into the dirt so the plant roots wouldn't get burned. What about worms?

She picked up a handful of soil and looked at it carefully. There were tiny movements. An ant pushed its way up and out of the dirt, then hurried purposefully across the surface of her handful, almost as if it had a mission. She closed her hand and buried it again, but when she opened her hand, it pushed onto the surface, undaunted. What had happened to its colony? When she put this handful into the hole, would the ant push its way clear back to the surface again, and could it find the other ants now that every bit of its world had been disrupted and rearranged? Could they keep their colony going? Would they have to start over? Would they just die? Where was the queen? Imagine a Kansas wheat farmer thinking about the fate of the ant colonies in his fields!

But there were all sorts of other things in the soil, too. As they'd worked this morning, she'd seen millipedes and cuddle bugs and beetle larvae. They'd uncovered cicadas, looking just like the empty skins she'd find during the summer, their backs split open where the adults had pushed their way out. But these skins weren't empty. They were full of cicada— sleeping, or whatever they did while they were waiting to change into adults. Not much beauty underground, Whitney thought. You'd have to be a cicada to appreciate that jointed hardness and those prickly legs. No peacock tails underground. Maybe that was why it was so easy to dismiss the lives of the underground world. Most of them were so ugly.

She went back to filling the hole, thinking about the ugliness of being underground. People didn't like being underground. Too dark, too damp and cold. Coal miners who worked underground all the time didn't seem to like it any better than anyone else. Of course, coal mines were dangerous. But just being underground, for people, was dangerous. It wasn't the world people were supposed to live in. Being underground, even in tunnels and mine shafts, was like being buried. And that meant being dead.

Still, here they were putting the root balls of the azalea plants underground and packing the dirt tightly around. For plants being underground meant life and growing. It was the opposite with people.

"Need a break?"

Whitney looked up to see Theodora, shovel in one hand, staring down at her. "No," she said. "I was just thinking about all the things that live under the ground. And about how we bury people there. When we bury plants, we expect life to come out of it. When we bury people, we know that it's death that wins."

Theodora looked away. Whitney had the feeling she'd said something wrong. It was almost as if a shadow had taken the place of the sunlight on Theodora's face. Without understanding why, Whitney shivered. It seemed that minutes went by before Theodora looked back at Whitney, and when she did, her eyes seemed to hold pain and darkness. "Perhaps that's why people plant flowers around graves. Maybe they think flowers, grass, trees, anything green and growing, can take away the power of death. Weaken it. Give the living hope."

"Hope for what?" Whitney asked. "A dead person can't come back."

Theodora shook her head. "No. Not the way he was. Not in any way we'd recognize. I think I mean hope in a more general way. Just—hope."

"Oh." Whitney didn't quite understand.

"Let's take a break anyway," Theodora said, "even if you don't need one. Between the rototiller and this shovel, my hands have just about had it. They're not used to working quite this way."

"What do you sculpt?" Whitney asked. "Wood or metal or what?"

"Stone. Marble or granite usually. Would your folks mind if you came over to my apartment for lunch? Or do you do a big family dinner on Sundays?"

"No. We usually have brunch on Sunday and then nothing until suppertime. I don't think they'd mind."

119

"I'm renting a place a few blocks from here until the house is ready. You can call home from there to let them know where you are."

"Okay. Shouldn't I finish these plants first?"

"I'll help."

Whitney finished filling the hole and patted the dirt down, aware of Theodora working beside her on the next plant. The woman's fences were high, she thought, more like walls that you couldn't see through, except where there were occasional tiny cracks. Mostly, it seemed that what could be seen through those cracks was something dark and unhappy. And it seemed, somehow, to have something to do with her work. She didn't just not talk about it, she shoved the subject away. Whenever Whitney brought it up, Theodora switched to something else. If anybody thought she'd learn something about art or sculpture from Theodora Bourke, they were wrong.

Her mother was glad to let her have lunch with Theodora again. Whitney could tell that both her parents thought it was some kind of honor to be invited to lunch with a famous artist. Whitney, sitting in an incredibly comfortable leather lounge chair watching Theodora work in the tiny kitchen, wondered what her parents would think when they met her. Would they be disappointed? Would she live up to their ideas about what she ought to be like? She certainly wouldn't live up to Kate's. No dangly earrings, no artsy clothes. Just this very tall, very plain, very strong-looking woman who liked to garden and, apparently, to cook as well.

Theodora chopped green pepper and onions with sure hands, moving the huge knife on the cutting board almost as

120

fast as a professional chef would, Whitney thought. She compared that with the way her mother was in the kitchen, and grinned to herself. Practically the only thing her mother's hands were that sure about these days was taking something out of the freezer and putting it into the microwave. Anything that didn't come in a box or frozen or somehow prepackaged, pre-chopped, pre-prepared, hardly found its way into the Whitehurst kitchen in the first place. Marianne Whitehurst said that the only creativity left to her cooking was the decision about which package to open. It wasn't true, of course. Sometimes she would spend half the day on Saturday making casseroles that she could freeze to have during the week. But at home, lunch tended to be Cup-a-Soup and crackers or peanut butter and jelly. She couldn't imagine her mother whipping up an omelet for lunch as Theodora was doing.

"Do you like strawberries?" Theodora asked.

"Sure!"

"It's still a little early. These must have come from California. But when I saw them at the store yesterday, I couldn't resist. I bought a quart. I'd forgotten."

"Forgotten what?"

Theodora raised the flame under the iron frying pan on her small stove. "That a quart is too much for one person."

She broke four eggs into a glass measuring cup, tossed the shells into a plastic container next to the sink, and whisked the eggs quickly before pouring them into the pan, where butter was sizzling. She shook the pan over the flame, tilting it this way and that. After a few moments, she set the pan down and pushed the peppers and onions off the cutting

121

board into the pan, sprinkled a large handful of grated cheese over it all, and then began moving the pan over the flame again. She picked up a flat wooden implement like nothing Whitney had ever seen, and in a few quick motions, folded the eggs over the vegetables and cheese, and finally slipped the completed omelet out onto a plate she had set out on the counter. "There. I hope it will be enough for us. You can always have some bread and marmalade if you need something more."

"I'm sure that'll be fine," Whitney said.

"With the strawberries, of course. Come sit."

Whitney went to the small round table with a vase of fresh daisies in its center and sat on one of two bentwood chairs.

Theodora set two plates, two pottery mugs, two forks, and two knives on the table. "Take your choice."

Whitney realized that nothing on the table matched anything else. The plates looked handmade, the top one a deep gray-blue, with an oriental brush-stroke pattern in the middle, the one underneath a rusty brown. One mug was almost black with an elegantly curved handle and the other had no handle at all but pinched places in its shiny gray sides. Even the knives and forks were of different patterns. Whitney took the top plate, the pinched mug, a fork with a wooden handle and a knife with a clear plastic handle. She thought of the matched dishes and silverware at home. Anytime a set of dishes got too many chips or lost too many pieces, Marianne Whitehurst would replace the whole set, giving the partial one to the PTA thrift shop. She would never think of putting unmatched pieces on the table for a guest.

Theodora cut the omelet in half and slipped one piece

onto Whitney's plate, the other onto the rusty brown plate. "I like your choice," she said. "That's my favorite mug."

"Oh, I'm sorry. Do you want it?"

Theodora laughed. "No, no. I like them all, or I wouldn't have them. My trouble is I never can decide on just one thing. I see a mug or a plate I like, but I can't imagine having a whole set of them because if I did that, I couldn't have something else I liked, too. This way the table looks a little patchy, but I get to have more of the things I like on it. What do you want to drink—milk or iced tea or soda? I think there's some ginger ale."

"Milk, please."

When Theodora had poured milk for both of them and set a large bowl of strawberries on the table, she sat down and handed Whitney a plaid napkin. Another was already at her own place. Whitney took it and put it in her lap, thinking again of the contrast with home. Cloth napkins were for Christmas and Easter, not for using at lunch.

"It's all right," Theodora said, "I don't have any paper ones. You can really use it."

Whitney felt herself blushing. "Do you read minds?"

"No. Body language. I get the feeling you're a little uncomfortable. You don't need to be, you know. If I hadn't wanted you here, I wouldn't have invited you."

"Thanks."

"You're welcome. Now eat before it gets cold."

Whitney ate. Almost before she knew it, her plate was empty.

"Strawberries?" Theodora asked. "I made whipped cream last night. Want some?"

Whitney nodded, and soon her plate held strawberries with a huge dollop of whipped cream on the top. She grinned. "I don't think I've ever had the real thing before."

"Really?"

"Really." Whitney glanced around the small apartment. "You sure have a lot of paintings." Every wall held several paintings, all abstract, all done with the same intensity of color. Whitney couldn't tell what they were supposed to be, if anything, but their vibrant colors filled the room with life.

"Yes."

"You live alone, don't you?" Whitney said, then quickly took a bite of strawberries and whipped cream. Maybe she shouldn't have asked such a direct question.

Theodora didn't answer for a moment. When she spoke, her voice was quiet. "I do now. My husband died last summer."

"I'm—I'm sorry. I didn't mean to pry."

"That wasn't prying. It was a perfectly ordinary question. Besides, asking a question doesn't force anybody to answer it." Theodora took a bite of strawberry and chewed it very slowly, looking over Whitney's head at the painting on the far wall. When she had swallowed, she looked back at Whitney. "I have a tendency to avoid talking about it. I'm not sure why I told you, except that we're having the strawberries. He had a genuine passion for strawberries. We always had a celebration the first time I bought them every spring. I saw them at the store last night and bought them, expecting, somehow, to share them with him. That's why I bought a whole quart, I suppose. It wasn't until I got home that I remembered— that I realized I'd be having them alone. I got them all cleaned

124

and ready, the cream all whipped, and then couldn't eat any. It means a great deal to me today to be able to share them with someone." She smiled again. "Someone who seems to like them almost as much as he did."

Whitney realized she'd already finished hers and blushed again. She must have been shoveling them in.

"I'm glad. You can have some more."

"Oh, no. Thanks. I mean . . ."

Theodora spooned more strawberries onto Whitney's plate and pushed the whipped cream container toward her. "Please."

Whitney spooned whipped cream onto the fruit. "Thanks. I'm never allowed seconds on dessert at home—sometimes I don't even get dessert. You've probably noticed I'm not exactly skinny."

"Do you consider yourself *fat?*"

"No. Or yes. I don't know. Other people do. My mother and my sister, at least."

Theodora narrowed her eyes and looked at Whitney intently. "Not fat. I would never say fat. Sturdy, perhaps."

Whitney nearly choked on her mouthful.

"You don't like 'sturdy'?"

Whitney put her napkin to her mouth, and finally managed to swallow. "It isn't that. It's better than 'fat,' for sure. But doesn't 'sturdy' mean strong?"

"Yes, in a way. Don't you think of yourself as strong?"

Images of destruction materialized in her mind again. Missiles and fires and mushroom clouds. Fear tingled along her arms and the back of her neck. Strong! "My dad says I tend to be hysterical. I—I get scared easily, I guess. Anyway, nobody's ever called me strong. I'm not."

"That isn't something we always know about ourselves. Even people who are sure they're strong may fall apart if anything happens to really test them. What kinds of things scare you?"

Whitney didn't know what to say. She didn't think she could stand to have Theodora Bourke laugh at her or dismiss it. "All kinds of things that other people don't seem to worry about."

"Who's to say they're right and you're wrong? And who's to say that fear is weakness? Sometimes fear's an entirely sensible reaction." Theodora ran both hands through her hair, which fell back into place exactly as it had been before. "I said my husband died last summer, and that's true. But it isn't the whole story."

There was a pause. Whitney had stopped eating. It didn't seem polite to keep on just now. The pause became a long silence. Then Theodora stood up, took her mug to the sink and rinsed it out. Was that all? Wasn't she going to explain what she meant? She opened the door of the small refrigerator, took out a glass container of water, filled her mug, and then stood with her back to Whitney, leaning against the sink.

"It was August—hot and sticky and terrible in the City. I decided to get away for a while one day, and went to a friend's farm in Connecticut. Andrew stayed to work at the gallery we owned. A friend of ours stayed with him. That evening, not half an hour before he would have closed up, some kids—some punks—looking for money chose the gallery. I suppose they thought it looked rich enough, classy enough, to offer a big take. They probably didn't even know what an art gallery was. Anyway, they came in and the leader pulled a gun and asked for money."

Theodora turned around, brought her mug to the table and sat down again. "Andrew explained that he had almost no money there, gave him what he had in his wallet and opened up the cash register to show them how little there was. Our friend gave them all he had, too. But they got mad. They were probably stoned or drunk. The kid shot Andrew. In the head." Theodora took a drink of water, and Whitney looked down at the napkin on her lap. She couldn't make herself look up, for some reason, couldn't confront that face. "He shot Tom, too—but only got him in the shoulder. After that they trashed the gallery. They broke the windows, slashed the paintings with knives, used sculptures as weapons to smash other sculptures. Nothing survived—except Tom. When they'd done, he managed to call the police. By the time I got back, Tom was in the hospital, Andrew had been taken away. There was only the mess of the gallery. And the blood. And the police."

Whitney didn't know what to say. "I'm sorry."

"Thank you. So was I. So am I. These last months have been like a test—to find out how strong I am. And the answer is, not very. Physically, yes. But physical strength isn't enough. I, too, get scared easily." She drained her mug and set it down. The sound was so loud, Whitney jumped. "I ran. From New York, from my friends, from Tom—who'd had the bad manners to survive. From the violence."

"New York must be a terrible place," Whitney said, remembering what Kate had said about it.

"That's what I thought." Theodora looked around the

127

apartment, her gaze resting on one painting after another. "Except that when you're alone and don't want to be, every place is a terrible place. The paintings on my walls are Andrew's. His work, living on, you see. But it isn't enough. Because the work isn't Andrew. You can't share strawberries with a painting." There was another long silence. "Sorry. I didn't mean to go on and on. I haven't yet worked out the questions about being strong and being afraid."

Whitney looked at her nearly empty bowl. All her fears were fantasy fears. What must it be like to have lost a real person? What must it be like to see the blood of someone you love and know you'll never see the person again?

"When you were talking about burying people and planting, I started thinking about what I'm doing these days, burying plants and knowing they'll live. Ripping out the weeds and the poison ivy and the creepers—that overgrown shrub—anything I don't want. Maybe I'm making up for not being able to rip the punks—the violence—out of New York."

Whitney remembered Jeremy bombing their block city and her reaction to it. "I don't think you can rip the violence out of any place. Or anyone."

Theodora gazed at her for a moment, then shrugged. "Maybe not. Maybe that's really what I'm afraid of." She stood, then. "Finish up and we'll go back to planting. Whatever the reason, I find it a good thing to do right now."

Whitney nodded. "So do I."

❦ 11 ❦

The sidewalk was familiar. Whitney knew she had walked it often. But there was something different about it, too. Landmarks had changed. There were trees she had never seen before, and buildings that towered over her—too tall for wherever she was. The differentness made her uneasy—not quite afraid, just uncomfortable. But she kept walking. She had something important to do, and there wasn't time to spend wondering where these buildings had come from or where exactly she was.

The sky was reddish pink where she could see it between buildings and trees, so it had to be early evening. Sunset. She walked faster. What was it she was supposed to be doing? Where were the others? Where were her mother and father, Kate, Jeremy? Suddenly, she knew what it was she had to do. She had to find them and warn them. They were in terrible danger, and she was the only one who knew. Whitney broke into a run, her feet pounding the pavement heavily as she went. It seemed almost as if the sidewalk had turned to something sticky that wouldn't let her move the way she needed to. She was running, but the faster she ran, the more slowly she seemed to go. The sky got redder. It was not sunset. Somewhere there was a fire. She could feel the hot wind from the fire on her face. She was running toward it.

She came out from between buildings and trees and found herself at the edge of a field that stretched ahead of her, empty and glowing in the reflections of massive fires that ringed the horizon. Above the flames, the smoke was a billow of purple and black. She was running more and more slowly now. The sidewalk had disappeared and she was trying to run through a tangle of vines and creepers that caught at her feet and scratched her legs. Finally, she saw them. They were having a picnic, sitting on a blanket spread out over the grass on a slight rise. Her father was sitting cross-legged with Jeremy in his lap. Her mother was dishing food onto paper plates, and Kate was playing her flute. Of course, Whitney thought. She forgot to practice this morning.

They were facing away from the fires. Whitney wondered how they could fail to see the color of the sky, or hear the roar of the flames. Couldn't they even feel the heat on the wind? She tried to call to them, but no sound would come. Suddenly, Paul was beside her. She gasped with relief. He would help. He would call to them. They'd hear Paul and come this way. Then they could all run to a safe place—a cave where the fire couldn't get to them. She stretched her hand out to Paul and he took it, smiling. Together, they stumbled on through the creepers. But he didn't call to her family. He made no sound at all. She turned to tell him that she couldn't shout, to ask him to shout for her, and the fear went through her like an electric shock. The person whose hand she was holding wasn't Paul after all. He was someone she had never seen before. His hair was long like Paul's, but he had a straggly mustache, the outline of a beard. He stopped

130

then, and when she tried to pull away, to keep running, he grinned like a Halloween mask and his hand held, not her hand, but a gun. There were three other figures behind him. She couldn't make out their faces. All she could see were their hands, holding silver guns that reflected the red light of the fires.

Those fires had grown now, leaping higher, had moved closer to where they all were. For a crazy moment she was glad. The fires would burn these figures, burn their guns, and she would be safe from them. Then she realized that her family was closer to the fires than she was—by the time the fires could save her, the others would be lost. She tried to see beyond the guns, to find out if her family had realized their danger yet, but couldn't. The air itself seemed to have grown both redder and darker. The figures in front of her seemed more sinister in the purple shadows they cast. They waved their guns and she became aware that she, too, held something in her hand. She looked down. The weight in her hand was a gun, exactly like theirs. She was safe. She could shoot them out of her way and get to her family. Maybe there was still time. She aimed the gun and felt her finger on the cold metal of the trigger. She had to shoot. Everything depended on it. But she couldn't. She couldn't even send the message to her hand. The gun was worthless.

Suddenly, in the sky above her, there was a flash of blinding light. A vast, circular ball of white formed in the sky, then turned yellow, then a dull, bloody red, blotting out the fires, the purple smoke, everything. The figures were gone. The gun was gone. And her family was there, directly in front of her, still sitting on the blanket, their faces lit by the fireball.

131

She screamed at them, and miracle of miracles, they heard her this time. They turned toward her and finally seemed to understand. Her father handed Jeremy to her, and then they were running, the fireball behind them. She had expected Jeremy to be too heavy for her, but he wasn't. She moved with him easily. Kate ran beside her, still clutching her flute. Her mother and father, holding hands, ran on her other side. Ahead, Whitney could see a ditch with water in it. Maybe they could get there. Maybe if they got to the ditch and threw themselves in, if they got wet enough, the fireball would go over them.

She glanced over her shoulder and the fireball was nearly upon them. Swirls of orange and yellow moved in the red center. Streaks of lightning flashed at the edges. They had reached the ditch. She looked to see if her parents knew what to do. The water in the ditch was their only chance. They weren't there. Kate, too, had disappeared. With a scream that felt as if it would tear her throat out, Whitney threw herself and Jeremy into the ditch. She put her own head under the water and held Jeremy down as the hot wind of the fireball overtook them.

Her own scream woke her. Her face was wet with tears and perspiration, and she had trouble catching her breath. Her room, cool and dark around her, didn't take away the terror. She could still feel the hot breath of the fire, the heaviness in her arms that had been Jeremy, the gritty water of the ditch. Her heart felt as if it were about to explode. She was awake, though. It had been a dream. She was safe. Except that she couldn't really believe it, couldn't stop crying.

"Whitney? Whitney, are you all right?" Her mother's figure was framed in the open doorway, silhouetted against the hall light. "Shall I turn on the light?"

Whitney tried to answer, but couldn't. Her throat seemed to be closed off by her tears. Suddenly the room was filled with the blinding light of the fireball. She squeezed her eyes shut against it.

"Sorry. Just keep them closed for a minute." Whitney felt the warm weight against her as her mother sat on her bed, and the cool hand against her forehead. "You're okay. It was a nightmare. Whatever it was, Whit, it was just a dream. I'm here now. Everything's okay."

"Is it? It doesn't feel okay."

"Bad one, huh?"

Whitney shuddered. "Bad."

"You want to talk about it?"

Whitney shook her head and opened her eyes just enough so that she could see her mother's face through her eyelashes. This was the face that had always been there when she'd had a nightmare, the person who'd hugged her and banished that lion that had haunted her dreams for so long when she was little. Why was her mother's presence not enough now? Why did the room, full of light, still hold such terror? What had changed—in herself? in her mother? Why didn't the hand against her forehead bring comfort anymore?

But she knew. It was the nightmare that had changed. It was too real. Theodora Bourke hadn't been able to wake up and find her husband still alive, the gang that had killed him only imaginary. Her nightmare was still going on. For her, a grown woman, Martinsville was like the ditch in Whitney's dream. It was a place to hide, a place to take everything you cared about and shove it under the water.

Marianne Whitehurst stifled a yawn. "You okay now? Can you go back to sleep? Or do you think it might happen again?"

"I'm okay." It was a lie. It felt as if she would never be okay again. The world was too terrifying a place to be, in spite of cardinals and squirrels, the planting of gardens. What good were gardens when kids had guns? When two countries, and more, were planning to destroy the world? What did the flimsy beauty of a peacock's tail have that could protect against the reality of the fear? "I'm okay," she repeated.

"You're sure? I can stay awhile longer if you want."

Whitney shook her head. "Go back to bed. I'll be okay. You've got to get up in the morning."

Her mother smiled, ruefully. "True. Monday—my favorite day. And I forgot to press a blouse last night, so I'll have to get up as early as the coffeemaker." She leaned down and kissed Whitney on the forehead. "Try to get yourself relaxed before you go back to sleep. Deep breaths. Do the rag doll exercise."

"Okay."

Moments later, in the darkness, Whitney tried to do as her mother had suggested. She thought of herself as a rag doll someone had thrown on the floor, with no muscles and no thoughts. "Rag toes," she said to herself. "Rag ankles, rag shins, rag knees." But the nightmare images didn't go away. She tried concentrating on her breathing, taking a long, deep breath, pausing, and then letting it out, slowly,

slowly, counting to ten, feeling her body flatten against the mattress as the breath went out. But in her mind was the fireball.

"Fill your mind with good thoughts." That was supposed to drive away fear, wasn't it? She thought about Raj, tried to picture his slow, quivering dance, to recapture her feelings when she'd seen his tail. She tried to remember the look of just one of the feathers. But it was no good; as soon as she could see that shimmering circle, it turned dark red and the fireball filled her mind again. Maybe the peacock's tail wasn't a map of the universe at all, but a prophesy about the end—a promise of suns exploding instead of circling safely in their eternal patterns.

When the first light of dawn edged her drawn blinds, Whitney was sure she had not been asleep again. She had spent the rest of the night reliving that nightmare, unable to drive any of the terror away. She got up and went to the bathroom, where she leaned against the cold edge of the sink and brushed her teeth. The round freckled face, surrounded by tousled, dusty red hair, looked back at her, no different than ever except for the tinges of grayish-blue beneath the eyes. She looked, she thought, the way her mother did before she "put some life" into her face with her makeup in the morning. She spat toothpaste into the sink and rinsed her mouth. Maybe it was fair that she should feel middle-aged today, at fourteen. It could be the only chance she'd ever have.

Back in her room, as she put on her jeans, Whitney decided to quit thinking. She would just pretend, as she had with her mother, that everything was all right. No more bugging everybody about her fear. It didn't do any good anyway, since no one wanted to listen, no one wanted to think about the end of the world. Maybe, if she tried hard enough, she could drive away the fear just by refusing to acknowledge it the way everybody else did. It couldn't be that no one else ever felt it. Anyone with half a brain had to be afraid sometimes. But the fear didn't paralyze anyone else. Not even Theodora Bourke. She gardened, didn't she? She had the nerve to pick up everything and move, to take on the project of creating a gallery, redoing the estate grounds.

Whitney had never lost anyone she loved. What right did she have to push her paranoia onto everyone else? If Theodora Bourke could put up fences and then manage to go right on living behind them, why not Whitney Whitehurst? When Allie came to pick her up for school, she'd ask about James Brady. And she'd have Paul tell her everything about his sci-fi convention. She'd ask to borrow that book he wanted her to read. He said it was funny. Maybe she could fill her head with funny things and drive the nightmare away.

There would be no more nightmares, that was all. She would build her fences and fill her life with things to do and think about, and the fireball would go away. It had to.

❦ 12 ❦

"Red, I think. It would be fantastic with your blond hair. Red or black."

Allie shook her head. "Whitney, red is too—sexy."

"Isn't that what you want?"

"Not from a dress."

"Black, then."

"Black makes people look thinner. You don't really think I want to look thinner, do you?"

Whitney took her sandwich out of its plastic bag. "I don't know why not. I do."

"So *you* wear a black dress to the spring ball."

"I'm not going."

"All right then. I am, and I want something pretty. Something pastel and lacy and feminine."

"Then why ask me? You already know what you want." Whitney took a bite of meatloaf sandwich and chewed it slowly. It was Thursday, and Allie had talked of nothing except James and the spring ball for four days. Whitney was getting very tired of both subjects.

"Don't tell me, let me guess." Paul joined them and plopped his lunch bag on the table. "The current topic is . . ." He pressed his hands to his temples and closed his eyes. "It's coming in. The clouds are fading and I can see it. The current topic is whether James will buy Allie Hamilton a corsage and whether, if he does, it will match her dress."

"Close, but no cigar," Whitney said.

"You two don't care," Allie said and gathered up her purse and her books. "Just because you're both cases of arrested development." She stood up. "Excuse me, but I just remembered a prior engagement."

Paul grinned. "Engagement? Has it come to that already? Don't you think you ought to wait until he has a job?"

"What about the rest of your lunch?" Whitney asked.

Allie glanced down at the table. "You can have it." Then she swept away, narrowly missing a collision with a girl carrying a cafeteria tray.

"Watch out!" Paul called after her. "Love is blind."

Whitney shook her head. "She's impossible. Does everybody get that way about their first love?"

"I don't know. I can't remember that far back."

"Oh, shut up and eat your salami."

"I can't shut up. I came over expressly to talk. Listen, Whit, while you've been serving your sentence in solitary, I've been doing some research. And I've got a whole batch of stuff for you."

Whitney bit into one of Allie's chocolate chip cookies. "What?"

Paul rummaged in his backpack, withdrew several crumpled sheets of paper, and smoothed them on the table. "Here. You can start with this one: The Committee for Nuclear Responsibility. It's in San Francisco. I don't have a phone

138

number for it, but you can write. That's too far to call, anyway."

"What are you talking about?"

"I'm telling you, Whit, there are a ton of groups you can join. I've got addresses and phone numbers and everything. There's the Center for War/Peace Studies. That's in New York. You can subscribe to their newsletter. And there's the Council for a Livable World—that's in Washington—and the Fellowship of Reconciliation—that's got a newsletter, too. And there's a Catholic thing called Pax Christi USA, and Physicians for Social Responsibility, and SANE—also with a newsletter. And the War Resisters League and Students Taking Action for Nuclear Disarmament . . ."

Whitney had closed her eyes. The fireball was there in her mind again. She tried to shake it away. "Stop it, Paul, I don't want to hear any more."

"You haven't heard nothin' yet! Guess what I've got here." He held up one of the sheets. "Guess."

"I don't want to guess. I want to eat my lunch and finish Allie's cookies and not hear about any more groups."

"This isn't a group. This is the best thing of all. This, Whitney Whitehurst, is the telephone number of the White House! Right now, if you wanted to, you could go to the nearest phone and call this number and the person who answers would be a White House operator. Honest! I tried it. I nearly died when she answered and said 'White House Executive Offices.' "

Whitney opened her eyes. "Are you kidding? Where'd you get it? You didn't really call the White House."

139

"I did. I honestly did."

"What'd you say?"

"I said, 'Please tell the president for me that I am very concerned about the proliferation of nuclear weapons and I think we should begin a freeze on production immediately.' I'd already written it out and memorized it." Paul grinned. "I actually called the White House and told them to stop making nuclear weapons. Of course, I didn't talk to the president. But I'll bet they have to make a note of everything people call up and say. Whitney, you've got to do it. It's a gas!"

"Where'd you get the number?"

"That's my secret. I've memorized it, though, in case there are other things I want to call about. It's a citizen's duty to let the president know where he stands. Here." He handed her the paper. "Area code two-oh-two, four, five, six, seven, six, three, nine. Right?"

"Right."

"So call it as soon as you get home from school. Make your voice heard, Whitney."

As Whitney looked at Paul, his face crinkled in the grin she'd known as long as she could remember, the dream came back to her. Paul's face had turned to the other one, with the mustache, the face of the man with the gun. The hair rose on the back of her neck, and she crumpled the sheet of paper held in her hand. "I don't want to call." She shoved the other papers back toward him. "And I don't want to join a group or subscribe to a newsletter or anything else. Just let me alone. I want to forget about it."

Paul frowned, then shrugged. "Okay, okay, don't get hyper."

140

He picked up the pages and put them back into his pack. "You know, Whitney, I think I'm going to swear off teen-aged girls. You're as crazy as Allie."

Until her two grounded weeks were up, Whitney went directly home after school every day. She spent the time while she was alone in the house getting ready for Jeremy to get home. She borrowed craft books from the library and gathered supplies, and as soon as he arrived, they began on one of the projects. They finger painted and made crayon-batik tee shirts, created bird feeders out of milk cartons and hung them in the backyard, put together a scrapbook with pictures of the birds they attracted to the feeders. They made a popsicle loom and wove a belt, they melted wax and made sand-cast candles. Everything she did with him was about making things, never destroying them. No more block cities that could be bombed, not even anything that would have to be taken apart and put away later.

Occasionally, when the weather was nice, she helped Theodora Bourke tear out vines and creepers, plant petunias and pansies and dwarf marigolds, line the flower beds with rocks. At those times, they worked in silence, as had become their habit, speaking only when necessary. When Raj chose to display for them, Whitney watched, holding her breath at the sight, never quite able to get used to it. But if the idea came to her that the circles on his tail might be exploding suns, she forced it away, singing inside her head the silly children's songs Jeremy had learned at day care until those thoughts went away. She got better and better at controlling the images in her mind.

141

Several times she almost asked Theodora to show her whatever was hiding under the cloths in the carriage house, but she always stopped herself before the words could come out. She was afraid that if she asked about those things, Theodora might let the fences down again, and she didn't want that. She didn't want to hear any more about guns and killing and blood, didn't want to think about death. Better just to plant and chop and prune and feel that comforting sense of togetherness they had working side by side, listening to the sounds around them. The azaleas began to bloom, and Whitney thought only about the color that came up from their roots and proved they were alive. If she ever began to wonder how long the garden might last, whether there would be other springs and time for the azaleas to grow the way Theodora wanted them to, she concentrated even harder on making things beautiful this year, today, now. She refused to consider the future.

To Paul's surprise, she borrowed the book he'd been pushing, and to her own surprise, she found it very funny. When she finished it, she borrowed the other three volumes of the so-called "trilogy." For the first time ever, she could actually talk to Paul about science fiction. But she didn't tell him about Theodora Bourke and the garden at the Old Place. And she didn't tell Allie either.

Her mother couldn't say enough about the projects she was doing with Jeremy. "You should look for a babysitting job this summer," she said one day. "You're getting awfully good with him. Maybe you could help out at his day-care center when school's out. They're always glad to have volunteers."

Whitney smiled the smile she found it easier and easier to

142

paste on. "Maybe I could." It might be a way to keep her head busy through all those long, empty summer days.

When she was no longer grounded, she went with Allie to pick a dress for the ball. She wasn't bored anymore with Allie's incessant talk about James. It was something to listen to, something to think about. She began to wonder if she'd ever feel that way about anyone, and tried to imagine feeling that way about Paul. It didn't work. Paul was definitely not a romantic figure. Of course, she thought when she was alone, James wasn't either, to anyone except Allie. Whenever Whitney looked in the mirror, she thought *sturdy*. That's what Theodora had said, and she was beginning to be that. She was no longer hysterical. The nightmare was gone. She smiled a lot. Sturdy people smiled, didn't they?

One warm, gray Saturday near the end of May, she was helping Theodora disentangle the old rose bushes near the gazebo. Theodora had bought her a pair of leather gloves that fit her better, and she was able to work more easily. Inside the gloves, her hands were getting stronger anyway, her palms tougher. She was pulling at a honeysuckle vine that had a long rose bush in what looked like a death grip, when a thorn pierced the leather of her glove and bit deeply into her thumb. She yelped, and Theodora looked up.

"You okay?"

Whitney nodded. "It's just a thorn. It went right through my glove." She took the glove off and looked at the bright drop of blood, that grew slowly as she watched. Suddenly, without even the slightest hint of what was coming, she burst into tears.

"Whitney? What is it? Are you hurt?"

143

Whitney shook her head, but she couldn't stop crying. It was as if the tears, the stomach-wrenching sobs, had been hiding somewhere inside, and the thorn had reached them, like a drill releasing an oil gusher. There was nothing she could do about it. Theodora took her by the shoulders and led her into the gazebo. She made her sit on the old crate and stood beside her, patting her awkwardly on the back as she cried. The sobs kept coming, and the harder Whitney cried, the worse she felt until it seemed as if no human being could hold so much misery. She doubled over, her head on her knees, and felt as if she might shake the gazebo down just by the sounds she was making, the terrible violence of her tears.

Eventually, slowly, the strength of the outburst began to fade, the sobs to slow down. She swallowed and sniffed, rubbed her wet face with her hands, and accepted the handkerchief Theodora offered. When she'd caught her breath, blown her nose, mopped away some of the tears, she looked up. Theodora was looking at her with that old darkness in her eyes again—the expression she was always afraid to see. It was not an Amazon look, didn't belong on that face. "I'm sorry," she said, finally. "I don't know what happened." She held up her thumb. The drop of blood was gone, and she could barely see the point where the thorn had gone in. "It didn't really hurt."

"Something did," Theodora said. "Something that's been hurting for a long time."

"No, I'm fine. I've been fine. It must have been the blood. Lots of people are afraid of blood."

"But not you." Theodora sat on the rock and rested her forearms on her knees, her hands clasped in front of her. She looked at Whitney in that intense way she had, as if she were getting ready to make a sculpture of her face. "You've been like a flower bulb the last few weeks, all hard and dry, with everything alive locked up inside. Since just about the time I told you about Andrew. Did that have anything to do with it?"

Whitney shook her head. It was the dream. But she didn't want to remember the dream.

"I hope not. I wouldn't have told you if I'd thought it would frighten you."

"It didn't." She didn't say what had frightened her. She would not think about it.

"When I first found you here and told you to come back whenever you wanted, you reminded me of myself when I was your age. You looked at things the way I did—as if you were devouring them, taking them inside you and making them part of yourself. You'd come here to try to see Raj again, because that one glimpse wasn't enough. But lately, it's as if you'd closed down, given up your eyes. You look, but you don't see. Last week when Raj was showing off for us, there was just a moment when I thought you were really seeing him, and then you seemed to catch yourself at it and closed down again."

"I was watching," Whitney said.

"Your eyes were on him, but the rest of you was someplace else. Have you ever seen a peahen when the cock is displaying for her?"

Whitney shook her head.

"All indifference. She looks anywhere but at that magnificent tail. As often as not, she simply walks away."

"So?"

"I have to believe that whether she looks at him or not, she sees. She's aware of him and she knows perfectly well that he's making all that show for her. In some other way, she's taking in every bit of what he wants her to notice. Otherwise, I suppose, peacocks would eventually quit doing it."

"I don't see what you're trying to tell me."

"They're the opposite of you. You look, but don't see. They see without having to look. Seeing involves a lot more than eyes. Something's happened to you, but I don't know what. A few weeks ago, you were one kind of person, and now you seem to be another kind. I don't believe this new person. Something inside you wants to see, wants to care."

The nightmare fireball took shape in Whitney's mind. "No! There are things I don't want to see."

"When we open our eyes we can't always choose what happens in front of them. Some of it's beautiful and some isn't."

"Then it's better not to see at all."

A starling uttered its harsh squawk in the trees overhead, and Theodora sighed. "When Andrew was killed, I wished for a while that he'd never lived. I wished that I'd never met him, never loved him, never depended on him and shared with him what was most important to me. I considered, for a while, selling all his paintings, ridding my life of everything that reminded me of him. You remember I told you once that you couldn't share strawberries with a painting? Well, I'm not completely over that stage of grief yet, I suppose. Sometimes I think I'd rather avoid strawberries forever than to face the pain of the memories they bring. But strawberries are still sweet, Whitney. When I ate those with you that day, they tasted as good as any I'd ever had with Andrew. When I'm thinking straight, I wouldn't give up his work, and lose my memories of him even to avoid the grief of having lost him."

"I've never known someone who died," Whitney said.

"Maybe not. But you act as if you're grieving, all the same. I don't know what you've lost or what you think you've lost. But I recognize those tears."

"Do you believe in God?"

"I suppose that depends on your definition. I don't believe in somebody you can pray to like calling him on the phone and asking for things. I don't believe in someone who controls our actions and decides, for instance, who will be robbed and killed and who will survive. But I believe there's a reason why roses grow. A poet named Blake said, 'The pride of the peacock is the glory of God.' Whatever *he* meant by that, I've always thought of the 'pride of the peacock' as its tail. Whoever or whatever designed peacock tails and roses also makes some of us want to create beauty ourselves. I can't believe that's an accident. I believe that's all 'the glory of God.' "

"But some people don't want to create beauty. Some people make weapons and rob and kill. Did God want that, too? And maybe it isn't just some people. Maybe there's that kind of violence somewhere in every one of us. Is that the way it's supposed to be?"

Theodora ran her hands through her hair. "I don't know the answer to that. For some reason there are two sides to everything—beauty and ugliness, life and death, peace and

147

violence, love and hate. Good and evil, if you will. What some people think of as God and the Devil. I don't know why. It's one of the questions people have been asking as long as they've been able to think."

"Well, I don't want to think about it," Whitney said. She looked into the woods behind the nearly cleared garden, dense and green now, dark beneath the overcast sky. "If you fill up your mind, you don't have to think about it."

"And have you been filling up your mind that way? Is that why you've quit seeing?"

"Yes, and it works. You can keep away the bad stuff."

"The way I could escape violence by running away from New York?"

"That's different."

Theodora stood up. "Why, if it's working so well, did you cry the way you did just now? Some things don't go away, they just hide. Pain and fear and grief are all like that. Don't let them fool you."

"We'd better go back to work," Whitney said, and handed the damp handkerchief back. "It's probably going to rain pretty soon."

"I've decided, by the way," Theodora said, touching the faded wood of the doorway gently, "to restore this place. When the garden around it is finished, it'll need something beautiful in the middle. This will give it continuity. The old, restored, adding its beauty to the new. Anyway Raj has taken to roosting on it every night. Who am I to question his taste—or to evict him from his chosen home, for that matter?"

Whitney grinned. "I'm glad. Oh, Theodora, I'm so glad!"

❦ 13 ❦

"Your mother said you'd be here."

Whitney, having just picked up an armload of honey-suckle vines she had torn out, nearly dropped them. She turned to see Paul standing beside the gazebo. He surveyed what had been little more than wilderness, now beginning to look like garden again, and whistled appreciatively. "Quite a change. You guys must have been working your heads off."

Whitney shifted the vines to keep them from slipping away from her. "More like working our arms off. You like it?"

"What's not to like? It wouldn't make as good a fort now," he said, waving at the gazebo, "but it would be better as a castle. Kings ought to have gardens, I should think. Of course it still needs a moat. And a fountain would be good."

Whitney carried her armload to the pile she had begun next to a newly uncovered stone path and dropped it. "Look at what we found. I'll bet you didn't know there were stone paths under all that junk. I tried to dig up a poison ivy plant and hit stone everywhere I dug, all around it. The darned thing was growing up through a crack. We started scraping all the leaves and dirt away and found the path. This one goes back to the house. We've uncovered the whole thing.

149

But there are some that go off into the woods, too. We've only started on those."

"Your mom says you've been working with this Bourke person for weeks. How come you never told me?"

"I don't know." Why had she kept all this to herself, she wondered. "I didn't think you'd be interested?"

"Oh, sure. I'm the one who found the gazebo in the first place. I'm also the one who told you about the newspaper article. Why would I be interested?"

"Okay, Paul. I really don't know why. First I was grounded . . ."

"Which naturally kept you from mentioning Theodora Bourke to me at school."

"No. But if you'd wanted to come over here after school, I couldn't have. You know, I wasn't allowed to do anything with you and Allie that whole time, but Dad said I could help Theodora. . . ."

"Theodora? You're on a first name basis with a famous artist and I haven't even met her?" Paul folded his arms across his chest and scowled. "Is that any way to treat a friend? A friend whose mother is a potter and dying to meet the sculptor?"

Whitney shrugged. "I'm sorry, Paul. I really am. She'll be back in a minute and you can meet her. She went to get the big pruning shears. And calling her Theodora was her idea."

"Well, I guess I could be induced to forgive you if you introduce me to her. Better late than never. Is that her?"

Theodora came down the path from the woods, carrying the pruning sheers in one gloved hand, and stopped. She looked

150

at Paul, took in the jeans with torn knees, faded blue tee shirt, long hair, and ratty sneakers, and frowned. "Is this a friend of yours?" she asked Whitney. Her tone suggested that she doubted it.

"This is Paul Forest, one of my best friends. Paul, this is Theodora Bourke, the sculptor."

Theodora's face relaxed. "This is the Paul of the fort and the castle and so on?"

Whitney nodded. Paul stepped forward, shyly for him, and held out his hand. "I'm very honored to meet you."

Theodora laughed, changed the shears to her left hand and shook hands with him. "I'm flattered. I can't remember the last time a teenaged boy felt himself 'honored' to meet me."

Paul grinned. "Well, I've only been a teenager for fourteen months. Maybe I don't have the hang of it yet."

"Or maybe his mother told him all about you," Whitney said. "She's a potter."

"And therefore weird enough to have heard of me."

"I didn't mean . . ."

"I know, Whitney. If you were to believe the newspaper, you'd think I was a household word. The fact is, sculptors hardly ever get to be household words, unless they're dead. You know, Michelangelo, Rodin. Not very many people even know Louise Nevelson. What brings you here, Paul?"

"Whitney's mother said I'd find her here, and I thought she wouldn't dare try to keep you to herself if I actually showed up. She's been keeping all this a deep, dark secret."

Theodora nodded. "So the truth is out. She's actually been working."

151

"A pretty shameful thing. I'm not surprised she didn't want me to know. In fact, couldn't there be trouble with the authorities? Child labor and all?"

"Only if I got paid," Whitney said.

"Voluntary labor doesn't count," Theodora said.

"Are you going to do this everywhere?" Paul asked. "Are you going to turn the whole estate grounds into a garden again?"

"It was never all garden," Theodora said, "except in the loosest possible definition. There were some wildflowers planted under the trees in some places, but a lot of it was left just natural woods. I intend to leave it that way, too."

"How about the Old Place? Are you going to tear it down?"

"Your castle? How could I do a thing like that?"

Paul looked from gazebo to the trimmed rose bushes. "It looks pretty ratty now that everything else is getting to be so elegant."

"She's planning to restore it," Whitney said. "It'll look the way it did when it was first built."

Paul grunted and shook his head. "It'd be easier to tear it out and do something else. I'll bet the supports are all rotted away. It would be fun to see it the way it was meant to be, though. Besides, if you tore it down, you'd probably get Whitney all hysterical."

"Why?"

"She's turned it into a symbol. You know—eventually, if you let it alone, it'll fall down. And eventually the world is going to end. Hasn't she been telling you about nuclear war?"

"Somehow the subject hasn't come up," Theodora said.

152

"That's funny. You mean she hasn't even mentioned Jonathan Schell?"

"Never mind, Paul," Whitney said. She wished he would shut up. "I'm not thinking about that anymore."

"I tried to get her to join the freeze movement—you know, circulate petitions and write letters to congressmen and all that—I even got her the White House phone number so she could call the president and complain. But she wouldn't even take the number."

Whitney could feel Theodora's eyes on her, though she didn't look back. "Paul, I don't want to talk about it!"

"I see," Theodora said. "What do you think about nuclear war, Paul?"

He laughed. "Oh, I think there's bound to be one someday. I mean, how can we go on making all those weapons and be sure we'll never use them? It could even be an accident. But I'm hoping that by that time lots of us will be living somewhere else. On another planet. Or maybe we'll have found out how to manage time travel. See, that way, we could jump forward in time and skip the war part. There was an episode on 'Dr. Who' where this rocket . . ."

" 'Dr. Who'?"

"Yeah, Who. It's a British sci-fi television show. Anyway, there was this episode that had a rocket full of bombs heading for the earth. They sent it backward in time so it wouldn't destroy everybody, and even though it hit, it got there before human beings had evolved and just destroyed the dinosaurs. That was a great story. Or maybe some other life form will come along and either save us or get everybody so paranoid

153

that human beings will just have to get together to fight off the aliens. It seems to me there are an infinite number of possibilities."

"That's because he's a science fiction freak," Whitney said.

"I resent the term," Paul said. "I happen to like science—and fiction—that's all. And anyway, I think you have to have a sense of humor about it all. Whitney has very little sense of humor."

"That isn't true! I think Douglas Adams is hysterical."

"Douglas Adams?" Theodora looked from one to the other.

"He wrote this great comic science fiction trilogy. That's what he calls it. So far he's done four volumes, though. He's British, too. I think they're funnier than we are or something. I don't see how you could read the Adams books and still be so gloomy about the end of the world." Paul paused for a moment. "Actually, now that I think about it, she hasn't been all that gloomy lately. Maybe working on the garden here has been good for her."

"Maybe," Theodora said. Whitney didn't look up. She felt as if Theodora's eyes were boring straight through her.

"Are you doing the house yourself, too? Along with the garden?" Paul asked, and Whitney was relieved to have the subject changed.

"No. I've hired contractors to get the gallery and my apartment ready. I'm only doing this as a kind of hobby."

Paul looked around. "Some hobby. It looks like a full-time job to me."

"Not quite."

"But when do you have time for your work?"

Theodora shifted the pruning shears back to her right hand.

154

"I've got a wisteria to attend to, and it looks as if it could rain any time. Whitney, if you'd like to show Paul the rest of what we've done, go ahead." Abruptly, she turned her back on them and went to work on the thick trunk of a vine that had wound itself around a young tree at the edge of the clearing and looked as if it might pull it down.

"What did I say?" Paul mouthed to Whitney.

She shrugged. "Come on. I'll show you the azalea gardens." Whitney led the way back toward the carriage house and Paul followed. Neither of them spoke until they were standing in the center of the driveway, surrounded by the neatly manicured azalea beds.

"That's some lady!" Paul said. "My mother said she was a good sculptor, but she didn't say anything about her as a person. I felt like a dwarf next to her. And nervous, too. Maybe because she's famous."

"Is that why you went on about me and nuclear war? I wish you hadn't gotten started on that."

"Sorry. I figured you must have been talking to her about it, you've been over here so much. But what did I say to her that made her turn off like that?" Paul asked.

"She doesn't talk about her work."

"Why not? From the way she acted you'd have thought I'd brought up the subject of social diseases or something."

"I don't really know. She's had a very bad year."

"Bad for her work or what?"

"Her husband was murdered."

"I knew that. Mom told me about it. A gang robbed their gallery in New York or something."

"Yes."

"But I don't understand what that would have to do with her work. Why wouldn't she talk about that? I didn't ask about her husband or anything."

"Maybe she's just so busy right now getting this place ready that she doesn't want to be reminded of how much time it takes away from her work."

Paul shrugged. "Not logical, Whit. I mean, she's got contractors fixing up the house. Why do the gardening herself? It's a tremendous job. And what if you hadn't come along? She'd have been doing it all alone. She wouldn't even have been able to get this much done by now. It doesn't make sense."

"So who says everything has to make sense? Come on, Paul, you're the one who believes in Vogons and two-headed hippies."

"An entirely sensible belief. And Zaphod Beeblebrox isn't a hippie. He's the President of the Galaxy." He pointed toward the carriage house. "Can you take me in there?"

"I don't know. She said I should show you what we've done. That isn't something we've done."

"Maybe not, but I'd sure like to see it. The newspaper article said she'd have a studio here. I've never been inside a sculptor's studio before."

"Well, it doesn't look like one, much. Her stuff's just sort of stored there. And there are covers over everything."

"So we look under the covers. Come on, Whit. Don't you have any curiosity at all?"

"Of course I do. But I also have some respect for other people's property."

"We're not going to hurt anything. I just want to see.

Theodora Bourke's a stone sculptor, for Pete's sake. How many of those are there? Most sculptors' studios probably look like welding shops. I don't even know what kinds of tools stone sculptors use. Except a chisel."

Reluctantly, Whitney led the way to the side door of the carriage house. It was standing open. If it had been closed, she might not have taken him in, but with the door standing open like that, it seemed okay. After all, she'd been inside often enough herself. It wasn't as if Theodora were trying to keep anything hidden exactly.

Paul stood for a moment in the dim light. Even when the sun was out, it wasn't very bright inside. On a gray day, the cloth-covered shapes loomed like undefined shadows. "Spooky, isn't it?" he whispered.

Whitney nodded. "Let's go. I don't really think I should have brought you here."

"At least let's look at something while we're here. Not that we'll be able to see much."

He crossed the floor, his footsteps echoing in the high-ceilinged space, and picked up one corner of a cloth. "Come here, Whit," he said. "Do you suppose she did this?"

Whitney joined him. Under the cloth was a sculpture carved out of marble. "What is it?"

"I can't tell. Feel it, Whitney. It's fantastic."

Whitney put her hand against the cold, smooth surface of the stone. It was hard to believe that anything as rough, as hard, as dense as marble could feel so—silky almost. "You couldn't say 'soft' about stone, could you?"

"I don't think so. But that's what I was thinking, too. Maybe it's partly how smooth it is and partly the shape.

157

Rounded like that. I wish we could take the cloth off and really see it."

Paul went to another shape. "This one's completely different!"

The second piece was not marble. Whitney didn't know what it was made of, but the surface was rough, grainy, and in places there were edges that were almost jagged. "Like a mountain," Paul said. "Or the Grand Canyon or something. I wonder if all these are hers or just things she's going to put in the gallery. These two don't seem to have been done by the same person." Paul let the cloth fall back into place. "Let's go ask her."

"I told you, she doesn't talk about her work."

"Maybe that's because you aren't pushy enough. Artists always want to show their work to people. That's why they're artists. Maybe it's just because we're kids."

"I don't think so. Anyway, you saw what happened when you asked. She just changes the subject."

"Persistence," said Paul. "It pays off every time. Let's go."

When they got back to the gazebo, Theodora had finished cutting away the wisteria. She was standing with her hands in her pockets, looking at the tree. "What do you think? That's a dogwood. Should I try to transplant it to the front of the house or leave it here? I hate to waste a dogwood where it's hardly seen. There aren't that many around here."

"I like it where it is," Whitney said. "If people are going to come back here when the garden's finished, they'll see it, won't they?"

"I suppose you're right. If I can just keep the wisteria from taking over again. It looks as if the darned thing was planted there on purpose. It must have been kept pruned back originally—the way some people do to make it look like a kind of weeping bush."

Paul took a deep breath and Whitney realized he was nervous again. "Are those sculptures in the carriage house for the gallery?" he asked.

Theodora turned away from the tree and faced them. "Yes. You couldn't have seen them very well. It must be pretty dark in the carriage house."

Whitney looked at the stones beneath her feet. She wished they hadn't gone in.

"We didn't really see them. I just peeked under a couple of the cloths. Mostly, we felt them. I figured the two we looked at had to be done by different people because they were so different. Are any of them yours?" Theodora nodded. "When is the gallery going to be open?" Paul asked then. "I'd really like to see them in the light, without covers."

"I expect everything to be ready by the end of the summer at the latest."

"Your studio, too?"

Before Theodora could answer, almost as if to keep her from answering, Raj stepped out of the woods with stately grace. He walked toward them across the paving stones, his head cocked slightly to one side. With barely a glance in their direction, he began to shake himself all over. Slowly, majestically, his tail began to lift and spread until it surrounded him in an arc of bronze and green and blue. As he always did, he turned away as soon as his tail was fully up. Theodora motioned to them to stand still, and they waited, while he seemed to display himself to the woods. His wings spread out to the sides and their tips drooped on the ground as he stepped forward and backward, dancing for an invisible audience. Finally, he began his slow turn. Even without the sun to catch the golds and bronzes, his tail seemed to glow. With one step to the left, he made it appear green. Another to the right and the color changed. He curved his neck and ducked his head, his delicately feathered crown quivering. Suddenly, he screamed. Again and again he did it, the sound seeming to spread out through the woods, bouncing off the trees and coming back just as a new one began. When he stopped, Whitney could feel the sound still vibrating in her ears and filling her head.

She couldn't tell how long he kept dancing, but it seemed, as he moved, that he might go on forever. He'd displayed often enough before, but never quite like this, Whitney thought. Then she realized she wasn't sure of that. It was as if every time it was something new, as if she'd never seen it before. Finally, shaking himself again, Raj folded his tail, turned, and stepped delicately back the way he had come.

"God!" Paul whispered. "God!"

"Exactly," Theodora said.

"Does he have a mate?" Paul asked.

"No. Peacocks have the unpleasant habit of eating flowers, and I don't want to raise them in my garden."

"No flower is any prettier than that! Anyway, you have *him* in your garden. Could it hurt to have another one?"

Theodora looked off in the direction Raj had gone. "You think he ought to have a mate, do you?"

"Don't you?"

"To tell you the truth, Paul, I hadn't even thought about it."

A low rumble of thunder filled the air. "It's going to rain," Whitney said. "We should probably get home."

"Yes, you'd better go." Theodora looked up into the sky. "I think we have a few minutes yet. Would you help me take the tools back? Then I'd be glad to give you a ride."

"That'd be great," Paul said. "Will the peacock be all right?"

"Raj? I expect so. He's been out in the rain before. Let's get on with it. I don't want to take you home soaking wet."

❦ 14 ❦

Whitney sat up in bed, wondering what it was that had wakened her, and almost immediately had her answer. Lightning made brilliant stripes of light around the slats of her blinds, followed instantly by a violent thunderclap that seemed to shake the house. Rain was hitting the windows so hard it sounded more like gravel against the glass. There had been a severe thunderstorm watch in effect when she'd gone to bed, and this, she was sure, was at the very least a severe thunderstorm. As another flash of lightning came, the door opened and Jeremy hurtled into her room, landing on her bed with such force that it crashed into the wall and she was nearly knocked over.

"I want to sleep in here with you!" he announced, his voice shaking. Whitney thought he was holding back tears with every bit of nerve he could muster. Thunder drowned out the rest of what he said, and he threw his arms around her neck.

"Okay, okay," she said, and disentangled herself from his choking grip. "Why me? Why don't you go in with Mom and Dad?"

"Because Dad said I couldn't anymore. Dad said I'm too big to come sleep with them when I'm scared."

Whitney hugged her brother and moved over so there was room for him next to her. "I remember when he told me that. I used to have nightmares all the time."

"Am I really too old to be scared, Whitney?"

"No, Jeremy. Nobody's too old to be scared." She paused while thunder rolled across the sky. "This'll be over pretty soon, anyway. You'll see. Have you been counting?"

Jeremy shook his head. "You can't count. There isn't time. It's right on top of the house. The thunder comes as soon as the light."

The room brightened again, and Jeremy put his hands over his ears as a crash that did sound as if it were on the roof over their heads made Whitney jump. "See?" she said, afterward. "That one scared me, too."

"Is it going to hit us?" Jeremy asked.

"Thunder doesn't hit," she assured him, and didn't mention that lightning did. "It's scary, but it isn't really dangerous."

"If people don't get too old to be scared, how come Dad said I'm too old?"

"He doesn't mean too old to be scared, he means too old to sleep with them."

"Then what am I supposed to do when I'm scared?"

"Maybe he wants you to figure out a way to get unscared all by yourself."

"Well, I'm not old enough to do that!"

"It could be that you're just too big to fit in their bed. You're growing and growing and growing, you know."

"Maybe it's because I kick. He says I kick him in the

163

sack . . . the sackro-illious . . . or something. He says he'd have to wear armor to stay in the same bed with me. When I was little I didn't kick as hard, I guess."

Lightning flashed and he put his hands over his ears again. This time, there was a slight pause before the thunderclap came. "There," Whitney said. "You can start to count now. It's going away."

"Are you sure? Will it come back?"

"I'm sure. And it won't come back because storms only move one way. Once they're gone, they're gone." Whitney hoped that was true, and that there wouldn't be another storm right behind this one.

"Am I too old to sleep with you, too?"

Whitney shook her head. "Not if you can lie still. If you kick me, I might change my mind."

"Did you used to sleep with Kate when you were scared and too big to stay with Mom and Dad?"

"Kate and I used to sleep in the same room." Whitney hadn't thought about those days in a long time. "So if we got scared, we had each other." She remembered one storm when she had jumped into Kate's bed the same way Jeremy had jumped into hers. The two of them had cracked heads because Kate had been just about to jump across the other way. First they'd cried because their heads had hurt, and then they'd started to laugh, and by the time they remembered to be scared of the thunder and lightning, the worst of the storm was over. She'd forgotten how close she and Kate had been when they were little. The two years between them hadn't seemed such a vast distance as it sometimes did now. They'd even looked more alike then. Kate hadn't been as thin and Whitney hadn't been as—sturdy. But Kate had been enough older to seem much wiser to Whitney. Safe. A protection against whatever Whitney was afraid of. It was strange that she'd forgotten. She and Kate hadn't shared a room for years and years, not since Whitney had started first grade.

She remembered now that the change had happened on her sixth birthday. She'd been given a room of her own as a present. Six, her father had said, was old enough to start to be more independent. But the present hadn't been as happy a present as it was supposed to be. There were those first few nights, when both she and Kate had cried. There had been nobody to talk to when the lights went out, nobody to share stories with, to joke with, to play scary games with, and then to cling to when they'd both gotten terrified. She'd liked the way her new room was decorated, and she'd liked having everything in it belong entirely to her, but she'd missed Kate terribly at first. That must have been, she thought, the beginning of the change that had pulled the two of them apart. Jeremy, she realized, had never had such a companion. She hugged him again, more tightly.

"Ouch, Whitney, you're squeezing me!" he protested. "Are you scared again?"

Whitney laughed. "No. Are you?"

Jeremy thought for a moment before he answered. "Yes, I am. I don't like storms and I don't want them to happen. Why do they happen?"

Whitney ruffled his hair. "I don't know why, Jeremy, they just do."

165

"Does God like to scare little kids?"

"Why would he want to do that?"

"I don't know, but I don't see why he makes storms if he doesn't want to scare us."

"Growing things need rain," Whitney said.

"But they don't need thunder and lightning. If they need rain, God could just make it rain. You know, the way it comes down sometimes and is fun to play in."

Whitney sighed. "Maybe God doesn't do every single thing that happens. Maybe storms and thunder and lightning happen just by themselves."

"That isn't what Mrs. DeMarco says at day care. She says God does every single thing."

Thunder rumbled across the sky again, but it wasn't as loud. The lightning was now an intermittent flickering. "I guess I just don't believe Mrs. DeMarco," Whitney said. "And you don't have to, either. Nobody knows for sure about God."

Jeremy yawned. "Are you sure I don't have to believe her about God?"

"I'm sure."

"Good. Because I didn't think I liked God very much. Whitney?"

"What, Jeremy?"

"Are there lots and lots of things you're scared of, or only just loud thunder sometimes?"

Whitney sighed. "Yes, Jeremy, there are lots and lots of things I'm scared of."

"And are you old enough to get unscared all by yourself?"

166

"No."

He yawned again and snuggled closer to her. "Good. Then I don't have to, either." He put his head down on her pillow. "Whitney?"

"What?"

"I'm glad you think God doesn't do every single thing. I'm glad he didn't make the world such a scary place on purpose."

"Me too."

He closed his eyes then, and turned over so he was curled with his back against her. "I'll try not to kick."

"Okay."

"Good night, Whitney. I'm glad you're here."

"Good night, Jeremy. I'm glad you're here, too."

Whitney rested on one elbow and watched his face soften as he relaxed into sleep. She was almost overwhelmed, suddenly, with love for him. She was glad he was here, even if he might kick. And she was glad she had Kate, even if they had grown apart. She didn't want to forget again how it had been when they were little. And her mother, who came, even now, to comfort her when she had a nightmare and who might dismiss her fears, but never told her she shouldn't have them. And her father, too, who thought a boy Jeremy's age should be able to get over being afraid all by himself, and who thought fear of nuclear war was foolish, but who at least *tried* to give her something to hope for, even if it wasn't enough.

She yawned, and slipped down so that she was lying curved around Jeremy. The thunder was little more than a faint

167

grumbling now. Another storm had passed, and lightning hadn't hurt them or their house. Was that God's doing or was it luck?

Theodora had talked about seeing and being open. Jeremy, lying so peacefully next to her, was open to anything. And sometimes he got scared. But it seemed almost as if he didn't mind, as long as there was somebody to crawl into bed with, somebody who would comfort him, as long as he didn't need to get unscared all by himself.

She thought of Theodora, alone in her small apartment. You had to be even stronger than an Amazon, she supposed, if you had nobody to comfort you. And that made her think of Raj. Had he been out in the storm? Could he have survived? She thought of him taking refuge in the gazebo, with the wind and rain and hail coming through the roof and the broken lattice sides. The first thing in the morning, she decided, she'd go look for him. If God didn't control thunder and lightning, He probably didn't look after peacocks either. She hoped Raj could look after himself.

Jeremy moved in his sleep and she put her arm across his shoulders. She didn't even care if he kicked.

❦ 15 ❦

By six-thirty the next morning, Whitney had abandoned her
bed. Jeremy didn't just kick, he squirmed, rolled, twisted,
and hit. She wondered how he could be rested and ready to
face a new day after thrashing around so much all night. No
wonder their father had had enough. Now Jeremy lay on his
back in the exact center of her bed, one arm flung up over his
head, the other stuck out over the edge. One knee was bent
so that his body had a slight twist in the center, and the other
leg was straight, stretched out in the opposite direction. Nothing larger than a guinea pig could share the bed with him
that way, Whitney thought.

Her alarm clock was blinking twelve midnight. The power
must have gone out during the storm. She checked her watch
and reset the clock, then looked out into the backyard. The
sun had risen in a nearly cloudless sky. Looking up, she might
think the storm had never happened. But looking anywhere
else, there was no doubt that it had been every bit as ferocious
as it had sounded. Branches, some with leaves still clinging
to them, had been blown down off the trees. A huge limb had
fallen across the fence and bent it nearly in half. The garbage
cans, which luckily had been empty, were lying on their sides

against the fence. The irises were battered to the ground. There were puddles everywhere.

Whitney dressed quickly, went down to the kitchen, and fixed herself a piece of toast and a glass of juice. She'd go over to the Old Place right away to find out whether Raj had survived the storm. The digital time display on the microwave was blank. She set that, too, grabbed her jacket, and started out the door. Then she stopped and went back to the memo board on the refrigerator. "Gone to see if the peacock was hurt. Back soon," she wrote, and signed it with a looping "W."

Evidence of the storm was everywhere as she walked to the Old Place. In one yard a full-sized tree had fallen, digging up half the lawn as its roots pulled free. The people were lucky, she thought as she passed the house, that it had just missed their garage. There wouldn't have been much left of it, or of the car inside. Though the electricity was on again, one traffic light was out, hanging useless above an intersection. There was no traffic yet, but if someone didn't fix it, there would be trouble at that corner when it was time for people to go to church.

The trees that were flowering had lost most of their blossoms, and everywhere flowers, like the irises in her backyard, had been bent to the ground. They'll come back, she assured herself as she hurried on. They're just hurt a little, not killed. She hoped Raj was no worse off than that, but she was beginning to be afraid. Instead of going through the broken fence, and having to make her way through the wet woods, she went around to the front of the estate and walked down the driveway. To her surprise, the van was there already.

170

Theodora must have been worried, too, she thought. Like the flowering trees, the azaleas had taken a beating. Most of their flowers lay scattered on the mulch. She went to the carriage house first, to see if Theodora might be there, but the door was closed and locked. As she started down the path toward the gazebo, she heard noises that sounded like someone stacking lumber.

What she saw when she emerged into the garden made her stop short. The gazebo was no more. Where it had stood there was a mass of splintered wood, chunks of roof with shingles still in place, broken boards with huge nails protruding. Theodora, bare-handed, was pulling at the pile, throwing broken slats and boards behind her. "Did you happen to see Raj as you were coming?" she asked when she looked up and saw Whitney. "I haven't been able to find him."

"No," Whitney said. "That's why I came over. I wanted to see if he'd gotten through the storm all right."

"Well, your guess is as good as mine." Theodora stood for a moment, surveying the wreckage. "It's my confident belief that he is not under here," she explained. "But I decided to be sure. You want to help?"

"I guess so," Whitney said. But she couldn't help thinking that if Raj *were* under there, she didn't want to know it. And she certainly didn't want to find him there. "Shouldn't you have gloves on? Those nails look dangerous."

"Yes, I should. When I got here and found this, I didn't think about anything but whether that fool bird had decided to take shelter inside it last night." She reached into her pocket, and tossed a set of keys to Whitney. "Get my gloves,

171

and yours, too, would you please? And bring a hammer and saw. The axe, too. Some of these pieces of the roof are too big to lift without breaking them up some more."

As Whitney did what Theodora had asked her to, she tried not to think about Raj. If Theodora couldn't lift some of the wreckage, a bird couldn't still be alive underneath. She remembered, suddenly, that many of the deaths in a city during a nuclear attack would come when people were crushed to death as buildings fell in. It hadn't seemed as dreadful a way to die as being vaporized or burned to death or dying of radiation poisoning. Now she wasn't so sure.

When she'd given Theodora her gloves and was putting on her own, she made a face. "Do you think I can help move this stuff without looking? This is one of those times I don't think I want to see everything there might be to see."

"I don't think you'd be much help with your eyes closed," Theodora said. "And you'd be very likely to get a nail through your glove like that thorn the other day. Tetanus is pretty ugly, too, you know."

"What if . . . ?"

"I know. What if we find him?" She sighed. "At least we'll know for sure. It'll be a terrible thing to see, but if he's dead, Whitney, he's dead. Not seeing wouldn't bring him back."

"I guess not, but I still don't want to have that to re-member."

"Tell you what. I'll look very hard, and if I see the slightest sign that he might be there, I'll tell you and you can leave. How's that?"

"What if I see him first?"

"Whitney, I've told you, I don't really think he's here. I

172

think he's probably somewhere perfectly safe, flashing his tail at some unsuspecting mourning dove."

Whitney forced a smile. "Okay. I just hope you're right."

"So do I."

They worked for a while in their customary silence, pulling out bits they could manage to extricate without moving the larger pieces.

"Well," Theodora said, tossing a gridwork of lattice pieces onto the stack behind her. "Was Paul right? Is the gazebo really a symbol for you? Are you traumatized now that it's gone?"

Whitney stopped tugging at a board that was refusing to come loose and thought about it. "I don't think so. I'm a lot more worried about Raj than I am about the Old Place."

"Good. The gazebo was only wood, after all, not a person."

Whitney laughed. "And Raj *is*? A person?"

"More or less."

"What about you? Aren't you traumatized? You'd decided to restore it."

Theodora stood for a moment, holding a bit of lattice from which the paint had flaked away, leaving it dull silvery gray. "That's very strange, Whitney. I'd have felt bad a few days ago, when I first decided to restore it. But I've been doing some thinking since then, and now I think I'm rather glad the decision has been made for me."

"Why?"

"Because I have a different idea about what to do here." She looked around the garden. "In fact, I have a lot of different ideas."

"Like what?"

"I'll tell you later. Meantime, tell me about nuclear war."

"What?"

"Paul says you have an obsession. Is that what made you turn off and quit seeing?"

Whitney nodded. "Other people don't worry about it—I can't even get people to admit they ever think about it."

"Most people don't. Or, if they do, they put it out of their minds as soon as possible. It's too terrifying."

"But the more people ignore it, the less they're really protected. I mean, if they just say they don't think it can happen, while we go on building more and more bombs and missiles and everything, then nuclear war just gets more and more likely. And so does extinction."

Theodora tried to lift a bit of roof, gave up, and pulled some more latticework away instead. "If you refuse to join any of the groups that're trying to make a difference, isn't that the same thing?"

"I suppose so. But joining a group would mean I'd have to think about it *all the time,* and I didn't want to have to do that. It's just that I was so scared . . ."

"Past tense? What about now?"

"I don't know. I thought I wasn't so scared any more, but I still am, I guess. You were right about the way I cried yesterday when that thorn stuck me. I'd been kidding myself that I could just pretend and make the fear go away. But last night during that storm, my little brother, Jeremy, came in to sleep with me because he was scared, and he said he couldn't get unscared all by himself. I thought about that, and I decided I couldn't either."

Theodora shook her head. "I'm not sure anyone can."

"I decided maybe I would join one of those freeze groups after all. It'll make me think about it even more, but at least I'll know I'm trying to do something. I got to thinking how important my family is to me, and Paul, and my friend Allie. And you."

"Thank you."

"Anyway, I thought maybe I could try to do something, whether it could work or not. At least I could try. And if it doesn't work—I mean if the world is going to end, at least I have the people I care about." She looked around at the garden and the woods. "And all this."

"And yourself. Don't forget yourself. Do you know Simon and Garfunkel?"

"The singers? My mom and dad have some of their records."

Theodora shook her head. "You make me feel old. They have a song called 'Bridge Over Troubled Water.' Do you know it?"

"Mom and Dad have that album."

"Listen to the words of the title song carefully sometime. There's one verse in particular—'When darkness comes, and pain is all around, like a bridge over troubled water, I will lay me down.' People can do that for each other, you know, Whitney. Sometimes, when the waters are troubled enough, other people are all you have."

"That's sort of what I was thinking last night." She grinned. "Of course, when my brother slept with me, I found out that other people can kick you, too."

"Well, nobody's perfect."

Whitney tried to pull a shattered beam loose from the

175

pile, but it wouldn't budge. They would have to begin breaking up the big roof pieces if they were to get much farther. She tried lifting it, using it as a lever, but it was too heavy. She dropped it and the pile shifted slightly. Whitney gasped. A peacock tail feather, wet and tattered, lay on the stone floor, just visible beneath the beam. "Theodora!"

Theodora, her face grim, knelt and touched the feather. "Now is the time to look away if you're going to." She stood up, grasped the beam Whitney had been trying to move, and alternately lifted up on it and pushed it down. Little by little the movement began shifting the mass above it. "Like a giant game of pick-up sticks," she muttered. "Except I want everything to move."

Whitney had put her hands over her eyes, but as Theodora grunted and strained at the beam, she went to help. "Maybe together, we can do it."

"Right."

The air seemed to be growing warmer around them as they worked, and the sun, early as it was, felt hot on their shoulders. Whitney could feel sweat trickling down her sides and back. As the beam began to move more freely, they began circling it until finally, with a crash that echoed back at them from the surrounding trees, the roof toppled sideways and the beam came loose, nearly sending them both to the ground. Theodora knelt again, both knees in a puddle. She pulled lattice and support boards away, tossing them behind her. She turned to Whitney then, and grinned. "It's just a feather," she said. "Just a feather." She pulled it out and held it up. Its spine was broken, so it flopped over and dangled, its bronze and blue sun, in spite of the wet, glowing in the light.

"Do you think he might still be under there anyway?" Whitney asked.

Theodora didn't have to answer. The garden's stillness was shattered by a raucous cry. It was repeated twice more, as Whitney and Theodora turned toward the sound. Moments later, stepping with his usual majesty, his bedraggled tail held carefully above the wet ground, Raj emerged from the woods. If he saw them or the wreckage of his chosen roost, he made no sign. He walked right past them and down the path toward the carriage house, his crown jiggling as he went.

Theodora laughed. "It's his breakfast time. Neither rain nor hail . . ." She paused.

". . . nor smashed gazebos . . ." Whitney continued.

". . . shall stay this peacock from his appointed food. We could have saved all this trouble and just waited for him to show up for his grain." Theodora looked down at her wet jeans, the broken feather in her gloved hand, then at Whitney, whose hair was stuck to her cheeks with perspiration. "Do you feel the faintest bit ridiculous?"

Whitney nodded. And then they were both laughing. As if in answer, Raj shrieked again. "I don't think he thinks it's funny," Whitney said, when she could get her breath.

"Peacocks lack a sense of humor. Grab the hammer and saw again, would you?" She started after the peacock and then stopped and turned back to Whitney. "I should tell you that one of the changes I've decided to make around here has to do with Raj."

"What is it?"

"I've decided your friend is right. Raj should have a wife. Maybe peacocks are as important for my garden as flowers."

Whitney looked at the glowing sun on the broken feather Theodora still held. "Maybe they are."

❦ 16 ❦

Raj, apparently unmoved both by the terrible night he had just survived and by the news that he would be acquiring a wife, ate his breakfast impassively and went off to display his tail among the battered azalea plants.

"He doesn't even care if there's anyone to see him, does he?" Whitney asked.

Theodora shook her head. "I think he has supreme confidence that what he has to offer the world is important. If the world doesn't notice or appreciate it, that's the world's problem. Maybe that's what Blake meant by pride."

Whitney giggled. "Paul's like that. Oh, I don't mean that he shows off or struts around like Raj. I just mean that when people tease him about his clothes or the way he wears his hair or something—or his brain—he just laughs it off."

"His mother's an artist. They do tend to be unconventional, you know. Maybe he inherited that."

Whitney nodded. "He gets the way he is about clothes and stuff from her. She lives in overalls that are covered with clay. I've never seen her in a dress. And you should see their house. Paul says they're going to clean it someday—really clean it. But I don't believe him. Every so often they pick some of the stuff up and shove it into a closet or something.

That's about it. My mother would have a heart attack if she had to live there. Paul and his mother don't have much money, so it's just as well they don't care about what they wear. But she's a terrific potter. At least I think so."

"I'd like to meet her."

"She'd like to meet you, too."

Theodora picked up the sack of feed and opened the carriage house door. "I brought a thermos of tea when I came this morning; would you like some?"

"Please."

While Theodora put away the bird feed and got the tea, Whitney walked among the covered shapes. "May I look at these?" she asked.

"After we've had our tea, we'll take the covers off."

"Why do you keep them covered?"

"Partly to keep the dust and dirt off them, partly to keep from having to look at them."

"Why?"

"Come get your tea."

They sat on the upturned crates at the workbench that had become their table, and sipped their tea. "This doesn't taste like anything I've ever had before," Whitney said. "What is it?"

"Do you like it?"

"Very much."

"It's blackberry. I find it comforting. Last night, during the storm, I wanted some comfort."

"You too?"

"Me too."

"Did the tea help?"

"Something did." Theodora smiled. Whitney thought she looked like an Amazon still, but softer somehow, like that marble sculpture. "Maybe it was Raj," Theodora said, "or maybe it was Paul asking questions, or maybe it was you. Probably it was a combination of all three."

"Me?"

"You. It was so easy for me, the other day, to tell you how you'd changed, so easy for me to see it. But I didn't make the connection then. When Paul asked me when the studio would be ready, so I could get back to work, I tried not to hear the question. I've been refusing to hear what my friends have been saying since I gave up the gallery in New York and moved here."

"What have they been saying?"

"That I'm hiding. Running away."

"But you told me that yourself, that you were running away from the violence in the city."

Theodora looked over Whitney's head toward the shrouded shapes behind her. "Not just from the violence. From myself, and my work. I've spent most of my life trying to make beautiful things. Suddenly, when those boys smashed the gallery and killed Andrew, there didn't seem to be any point to it anymore. What good was any bit of beauty I could create in a world like that, when a person's life could be snuffed out and the art he cared about smashed out of existence in a few minutes?"

"But the gardening—that's creating beauty, isn't it? You've been doing that."

"I know, and I wouldn't want to dismiss that kind of beauty. But it isn't the same thing. When you garden you

181

aren't really *creating*. You can choose colors and design the garden, but the plants have to make the beauty themselves— by being exactly what they're supposed to be. A holly red azalea is just that. I only plant it and hope it grows and blooms. Art is something different. Creating art is like *being* the azalea—making the flower yourself, except that the artist chooses what the flower will be. After Andrew was killed, I didn't want to choose anymore. I couldn't see how my work could have any value in a world of such pain."

"Is that like wondering what good life is when there's death?"

"Very like that."

"But doing your work couldn't *hurt* anyone, even if it couldn't keep away the pain and violence."

"It has to do with the impulse to make art, I think. It's like lighting a candle in the darkness. The reason you do that is to push the darkness back a little. If you get to thinking the dark is too strong to fight, you don't try anymore. You begin to run."

"The way I was running when I filled my head up with other things."

"Yes."

"What does Raj have to do with it?"

"During the storm last night, when I was so worried about him, I realized I couldn't protect myself the way I was trying to. I bought Raj because he was beautiful. I had no intention of getting to care about him the way I have. He could have been killed last night, as you and I both knew—and we were both afraid for him. Maybe we could protect ourselves from caring, Whitney, if we shut ourselves down hard enough, but what we'll have left is a life that isn't worth living. Raj, out there a minute ago, showing that tail off to the bushes, doesn't wonder for a minute who he is or whether his tail is worth showing. Or even whether he can accomplish anything by showing it. He just does. He's a peacock. I'm a sculptor. I began to think, last night, that every day I spend refusing to do my work is a day I side with chaos and violence and death."

Whitney took the last sip of her tea and sat for a moment looking at the empty styrofoam cup in her hand. "And every day I don't join those people working against nuclear war is a day I side with war?"

"What do you think?"

"Yes."

"Gardening was something I had to do, and I don't regret having spent the time doing it. We've helped some beauty along, and we've been working for life. That's good. But it's time to get back to my real work. In a way, I've been denying who I am, just as you did when you tried to be a person who could live without thinking about the future. You tried to be the kind of person who could avoid fear by not knowing. That isn't who you are. And a gardener isn't who I am." Theodora poured herself another cup of tea and offered the thermos to Whitney. "Have you ever been so afraid that you considered suicide?"

Whitney nodded.

"But you didn't kill yourself."

"No."

"I began to suspect that avoiding who you are is a kind of suicide. It's siding with death."

183

"Are you finding a wife for Raj to side with life?"

"Definitely."

"Will they have babies?" Whitney asked. "What do you call baby peacocks?"

"I don't know. But I hope they'll have them, whatever you call them. Wouldn't it be wonderful to come into the garden and find three or four peacocks displaying their tails?"

"But they'll eat the flowers!"

"That will be the gardener's problem."

"You're going to hire a gardener?"

Theodora nodded, smiling. "It's about time. I do love gardens, but I don't know anything about flowers that I haven't had to look up in one of those books. I know a great deal about setting up an art gallery, and even more about sculpting stone. And if I want some good hard exercise to work my body when I'm very, very sad, I can't think of an art form that provides more exercise."

"Paul will want to come see your studio when it's ready. He wants to know how stone sculptors work."

"I'll consider letting him in on the secret. Maybe we'll have a small studio-warming party. I'll invite you and your family and Paul . . ."

"And his mother?"

"Definitely his mother. She sounds as if she could become another friend for me here."

"Another?"

"Yes. You're the first."

"Oh." Whitney felt her cheeks burning. "Thanks."

"Why thank me? Don't you think of me as a friend?"

"Well—yes, I guess so."

184

"Good. Who else should I invite?"

"My friend Allie'd like to come. And maybe her boyfriend. That's all."

"Excellent." Theodora capped the thermos and stood up. "Shall we have a brief tour of what's here now? You know, when I saw that mess in the garden this morning, I have to confess my first thought wasn't for Raj's safety. My first thought was that without the gazebo, the garden was a perfect place for a particular piece of stone I found just before Andrew died. It's down there on the end. It'll take some work, of course, because it's just the stone right now."

Whitney drained her cup and put it on the workbench. She would miss the gardening, she thought. "Maybe I could help your gardener sometimes," she said.

"In that case, you'd better help me pick one. I'll advertise for a gardening pacifist, how's that?" Theodora reached for the cloth covering the first sculpture. "Two of these are mine, the others are by friends. Let's see if you can guess which are which."

She pulled the cover off the marble piece Whitney had touched. It was taller than Theodora, and though it was an abstract form, it could only be a pregnant woman, all curves and roundness. In the pale sunlight streaming through a high window, the smoothly polished marble glowed as if it were alive. Whitney grinned. She had no doubt at all. "You did this one," she said.

185